# Grandma's Cookbook Final Revelations

Pukka Carpenter

*AuthorHouse™ LLC*
*1663 Liberty Drive*
*Bloomington, IN 47403*
*www.authorhouse.com*
*Phone: 1-800-839-8640*

*Published by AuthorHouse 09/26/2014*

*ISBN: 978-1-4969-4119-0 (sc)*
*ISBN: 978-1-4969-4120-6 (e)*

*Library of Congress Control Number: 2014916952*

*Any people depicted in stock imagery provided by Thinkstock are models,*
*and such images are being used for illustrative purposes only.*
*Certain stock imagery © Thinkstock.*

*This book is printed on acid-free paper.*

*Because of the dynamic nature of the Internet, any web addresses or links contained in this book may have changed*
*since publication and may no longer be valid. The views expressed in this work are solely those of the author and do not*
*necessarily reflect the views of the publisher, and the publisher hereby disclaims any responsibility for them.*

authorHOUSE®

# Crimson Wishes.

While in secret you were born.
God chose your parts of perfect form.
Your first gleaming hoof touched the ground.
Somewhere on Earth a thunder sound.

Upon your head a star shone bright,
It will light your way both day and night.
Last two gleaming feet to Earth fell.
Strong pinions. They will serve you well.

You drink the wind with nostrils flared.
Will-o-Wisp can be seen in your hair.
Your strength and power grow stronger still.
Your speed and courage show iron will.

Oh, that I could keep you here with me,
But that is not your destiny.
Soaring over land and sea
To Homeland where you are free.

Oh, how I wish I could keep thee.
But all must see your quality.
Eyes will gaze admirably,
As you prance. Perfect symmetry.

With eyes of fire and spirit free,
You will capture hearts of all who see.
Although missed and far from me
Your presence lingers in my memory.

Earl F. Hartwig          Marlene Carpenter

# TABLE OF CONTENTS

# New Smyrna Beach

Left Albany International Airport Friday at 11:45 a.m. Landed in Daytona, Florida. Rented a fuel efficient 4-door candy apple red Plymouth Sundance. Drove to Ocala. Located destination point without major problems.

"Just grab small blue suitcase. Its live contents must remain cold."

"Ok dear. My sister should be home. Called last night. Ring their chime."

"Hi Carol, Pukka. Glad you experienced a safe flight. Please enter. Marlene likely returns momentarily. Went grocery shopping. Humph. Nearly three hours ago."

"Hello Jack. Thanks for letting us stay here until check-in time. Magnificent spread!"

"Our pleasure. Bring those mentioned fresh New England lobsters?"

"Absolutely. They weigh slightly over 2½ pounds each. Ice packed. Purchase this blue vault."

Moments later, bustling seafood donation squirmed faultily aboard bronze-colored refrigerator.

"Follow me to nearby sleeping quarters. Bathroom resides directly across hallway."

Unpacking consumed 15 minutes.

"Honey? Come socialize. Join brother-in-law's billiard tournament. Already lost both tactics. Going broke."

"What stakes we talk? Nothing expensive probably."

"$2 per game. Competing against resident hustler. Got change for this $20 bill?"

"Sure. Keep that money. Here. Grab all 12 singles. Now run along. Busy temporarily. Good luck."

"Thanks. Hurry."

Phone rang seven times. Almost hung up.

"Hello. Harold? Sorry about that. Althea was just leaving."

"Hi Grandma. We accomplished long journey without catastrophic accidents."

"Pukka? Did not expect this call so quickly. Where exactly are my neighbors situated?"

"Linpav's Arabian horse ranch. Marlene is not here yet, but due anytime. Impressive. Hmm. Totally awesome layout."

"When returning? Next month?"

"Yes. Late evening about 9:00 o'clock May 19th. Staying 24 days altogether. Checking into our ocean-front condominium day after tomorrow. Actually, not a very distant trek. We plan calling often. Keep Momma updated accordingly."

"Will do. Bring back some photographs."

"Bye, Grandma."

Scene ends. Reopens Saturday noontime.

"Delicious meal. Never even heard your term before. What label did Hubby fabricate?"

"Invented nothing. Merely followed Grandma's recipe listed under: Veal Oscar."

After lunch Marlene exercised her champion stallion while three of us milled around their screened pool area.

"Knew something was different. Just could not grasp exactly what. Bleached your darker hair hey?"

"Yes Jack. Stunned Hubby something wicked, but he always revels pleasant surprises."

"Care for beverages? Chianti wine? Only used half that colossal bottle steaming lobsters."

"Certainly. Would love some."

"Prefer beer myself."

"Wife enjoys Natural Ice occasionally. Frolic on diving board. Returning soon with refreshments."

"What kind of birds are those?"

"Vultures."

"Glad Massachusetts residents do not cope with giant flying scavengers."

"Have them also. Rarely see any though. Plentiful only during summer months."

"Lost all, but one episode last night. Jack plays billiards very well. Hope to improve some. Should have brought our personal cue sticks. Remembered everything else. Even recollected your Fenwick graphite fly rod, reel and assorted flies."

"Good job. Well, bourgeois has rebounded. Looks like big sister remembered she entertained company."

"No one cooks tonight. Instead we dine in South Daytona. Pukka or Carol can drive there. Not far really."

Landed at Duff's Buffet Restaurant. Brother-in-law insisted on paying all our low entrance fees. Fish baked and breaded, turkey, ham, roast beef, myriad salads, soups. Enormous dessert bar. Very overwhelming eatery.

"Just love it. Jack and I dine here two or three times per month."

"Some buffets exist back home, but nothing of this magnitude."

"Rejoining forces soon. Going back for delicious roast beef. Hmm. More fried green tomatoes also."

25 minutes slid by. Marlene and Carol returned from their second bout with various sweets.

"Staring at your empty plate?"

"Had plenty dear."

Sunday morning we departed. Headed east then south. Stopped for directions twice. Eventually crossed over New Smyrna bridge onto the island. Located condominium finally.

"Wow! Wonderful emplacement. Only 50' to ocean waves. Totally impressed."

"Glad wife approves. Best announce our presence. Sign over there behind us says 'Office'. Wait here."

"Good afternoon. Name please."

"Pukka Carpenter. Suite number two."

"Let me examine our logbook. That one is not ready yet. Come back later."

"What time?"

"1½ hours minimum."

"Alright miss. Any food markets close?"

"My name is Renee, your assigned caretaker. No businesses like that on this island. Several fine restaurants though. Interested in party boat fishing? If so, grab a card."

"Thanks."

"You are welcome to all amenities. Visit our next door recreation area. Free pinball games. Ping pong, darts, shuffleboard, billiard table, salt water fishing equipment, beach umbrellas."

"Flyer claims you have a swimming pool and sauna."

"True, but only available for registered guests."

"Been very helpful. Bye."

Returned to rental car. Twisted ignition key clockwise.

"Any problems Honey?"

"Arrived somewhat early. Need supplies anyway. Going grocery shopping."

Spent $62.88 - Winn Dixie and $63.09 - Publix supermarkets.

Scene ends. Reopens 2:15 p.m. in our Suite.

"Who are you calling?"

"Renee supplied an appropriate phone number."

"Hello. Deep sea excursions. Hazel speaking."

"Greetings Hazel. Would like to make reservations for two adults aboard Joy B."

"Booked solid until Tuesday."

"Sounds favorable."

"Captain Picket vacates sharply at 9:00 a.m. weekdays. $55 per person. Must pay up front. That by credit card?"

"No. Will be there shortly with cash."

Carol was occupied restocking large refrigerator.

"Leaving now, but relapsing within 40 minutes."

"Should have everything unpacked by then. Do not get lost. Oh! Want anything special saved out for supper?"

"Reserve bulk hamburger plus club rolls. Freeze everything else. Use your own judgement darling."

Six miles slid past. Spotted mooring area. Ambled toward main office. Only one woman seated at her desk. It had to be Hazel. Shelled out $110. Actually, only $10 cash and a $100 traveler's check. Found out cleaning of fish costs 35 cents per pound. (Undressed weight.) Also discovered our craft was wooden and 30 years ancient.

"Welcome home. Things progress beneficially?"

"Think so. Certainly shelled out enough cash. Still overpowering hot outside. Close to 100 degrees. Cool indoors though."

"Hooked up our answering machine. Getting hungry. Performing chef duties tonight?"

"Unnecessary. Gazebo cookout begins at 5:00 o'clock."

"Nearly that time already. Best hustle. Far away?"

"Guessing, maybe 60'. Condominium sponsors one free addressing new clientele every Sunday."

Small parking lot was full. 16 strangers milled around. Renee was only familiar face. Hostess appeared busy. We sat in molded plastic chairs.

"Go grab some food. Gas grill cranks."

"Want anything yet?"

"Negative dear. Content now."

"Absconding with chicken wings, potato salad, gherkins. Returning shortly."

"Hi Pukka. Meet Jimmy and his lovely wife Marge. You both hale from New England."

"Really? What state? Williamstown, Massachusetts here."

"Moody, Maine. My pediatrician husband wanted to get away from all that snow. Vacationing 14 days."

"Well, got to run. Enjoy your conversation."

"Extorting another cold brew. Ready Guavas?"

"Sure. Where do we dispose of empties?"

"Hand that over. Care for Corona light Pukka?"

"Supplied plenty. Thanks anyway."

"Renee claims you are breaking records. No one ever stayed three consecutive weeks before."

"Have some pickles Honey."

"Are they sweet?"

"Am positive sugar is involved. Not an excessive amount though. Try some."

"Yummy. Marge? This is my wife, Carol."

"Far from there. 150 miles west."

"Grab one of these bottles."

Scene ends. Reopens 10:05 a.m. Tuesday aboard Joy B.

"We doing something wrong? Using identical bait, yet catching nothing."

"Watch Jim. As soon as you feel contact with ocean's floor they bite. Set your hook. Then real in another."

Ship's mate, Joseph, weighed our 42 pound catch. Mostly Redfish, but three groupers, five black bass.

"$14.70 please."

"Apprehend this $20 bill. Keep any change."

In our condominium suite Carol froze over 30 pounds of succulent fillets.

"John F. Kennedy space center was impressive yesterday. Make any plans for tomorrow?"

"Calling my sister later. Telling Marlene to join forces here. Might investigate Disneyland."

"Want hamburgers again?"

"Arms are extremely tired darling. No one cooks. After showering, this team hits some nearby eatery."

"Welcome to the Steakhouse. Our afternoon special: North Atlantic salmon - blackened, bronzed, or grilled."

"Been around fish all morning. Will try your Caesar salad, eight-ounce coriander pork chop. Mashed potatoes, amaretto cinnamon apples."

"Same order plus double side dishes of Burgundy mushrooms and onion crisps."

Everything tasted divine. Price was reasonable. Excellent service. Left hefty tip.

"Answering machine blinks. Got a message."

"Althea here. Thanks for the astonishing plane tickets. You surprised us big time. Flying down there Sunday, May 6th. Well, later."

"Hello. John Linpav speaking."

"Hi Jack. Pukka calling. Went ocean fishing this morning. Successfully. Would Marlene be available?"

"Presently exercising young Arabian stallion. Expect her to return shortly. Yes. Here she comes now. Please wait one minute."

"What is up baby brother?"

"Aiming for Disneyland tomorrow. Was wondering if you and hubby could join festivities. Meet here at ocean side, planning a couple overnight visitations."

"Tonight? Hmm. Must think your proposal over. Condominium supplies adequate sleeping quarters?"

"Certainly. Went fishing today. Caught nearly 32 pounds of fresh fillets."

"Great job. Will call back after contacting hired custodian. Take care."

"Feel like strolling pristine beach?"

"Yes dear. Must change shirts first. Putting on another tank top."

Tide was out. White sand everywhere. Returned at 6:55. Phone rang. Issued explicit directions. Drove north to New Smyrna bridge. Waited. Finally recognized Sister's Cadillac. Jack was behind steering wheel. They both waved acknowledgement, then followed rental car.

"Require any assistance hauling anything?"

"No, but thanks anyway. Things remain under control. Only brought three small suitcases."

"Quaint little oceanfront bungalow. Where is our bedroom? Must unpack luggage."

"Straight ahead. Honey? While I show guests around, go get something tasty for supper. Do not get lost."

Ordered four Greek salads and a large combination pizza at Manny's Beachside pizzeria, then ventured back to awaiting condominium.

"Have done well voyager. Set out forks already. Oh! There has been plan changes. We visit Busch Gardens theme park tomorrow. Your sister supplied tickets."

"Disneyland is overburdened with various attractions for children. Epcot Center seems geared more for adults. We will take their boat ride across the lake Tuesday. Alright youngest brother?"

"Delicious Pizza. Salad tastes great also."

"Glad you like it Jack. Yes Marlene. Hmm. Where might this theme park be?"

"Tampa. We will take my Cadillac. Hubby drives his passengers there. Bring your camera."

Scene ends. Reopens Wednesday noontime.

"How much further? Walked miles through this desert."

"Look! Another chameleon."

"Who cares? What is that guy doing with his net?"

"Not sure. Probably capturing bait."

Returned at 4:30. Changed into swim wear. Investigated pool. Flopped aboard lounge chairs until 6:15.

"Another cold beer? Last one we brought."

"Ok. Where are you heading?"

"Getting hungry. Want boiled ham dinner?"

"Ok. Sounds wonderful. Coming with you. Must shave again anyhow. Neglected my razor this morning."

One message:

"Marlene here. Made safe journey. Had an excellent visit. Stop by our Ocala ranch before heading back north to Massachusetts."

"Hello."

"Hi Grandma. How are you?"

"Pukka? Been raining all day. Hope my grandson enjoys better weather. Am sure things are alright. Your sister called last night claiming your location manifests grandeur."

"Having super fun. Carol says: Hi. She is boiling ham now. Probably make hash for breakfast using leftovers."

"Been taking any pictures?"

"Certainly. Albino Bengal tigers, snapping turtle sunning itself aboard large alligator's head, sunrises, Carol holding stringer full of fish, Awesome Epcot Center, etc. See for yourself when we venture back."

"Be careful. Tigers can be extremely dangerous. They captured?"

"Surrounded by tall fence, but free to move around unrestricted."

"Good for them. Would never catch me swimming in the ocean. Sharks, stingrays, and only God knows what else live there. Stay on solid ground."

"Located an awesome tropical paradise today. Palm trees, orchids everywhere. Simply beautiful."

"Best wear sun block and sombreros. Marlene says both of you are turning red."

"Will do. Everyone carouses Cinco de Mayo here. Apparently, celebration continues all this month. Some type of Mexican war victory against French army soldiers that took place 200 years ago."

"Well, must hang up now. Your Dad knocks on garage entrance door. Keep faith."

"Ok Grandma. Bye."

After supper troupe attended recreation hall. Bought two sets of electronic darts. Tungsten. With cases. Mine weighed 18 grams. Wife selected their 16 gram variant. Cost $118 total including half dozen spare hard plastic tips. Played regulation for 90 minutes. As partners we won all but one tournament. Thursday both of us headed west. Explored Marco Island. Made reservations aboard another ocean craft. Returned to Naples Friday. Caught many sea trout, two Pompano, then angled for shark. I hooked into one massive ten foot Mako, but lost that hard fought battle. Carol successfully landed a mud shark that weighed over 320 lbs. Important people arrived Sunday. Picked them up at Daytona airport. Drove back to our bungalow. By 4:15 everyone was settled. Soon, Momma claimed her preferred seating location with spectacular views. (Ocean waves rolling toward shore.) Filled our 6-pack cooler. Exited through backdoor.

"Hey Guavas! Look who joined gazebo festivities. Good afternoon neighbors."

"Hi Jim, Marge. Pukka's parents arrived today. Meet Harold and Althea. Anyone care for cold Amstel light?"

"Unnecessary Carol. Supplied abundant Corona. Fantastic meeting your family."

"Go grab something charred. Free hamburgers, hot dogs, chicken wings, sausage patties, various salads."

"Only have the seven days remaining. Visiting Orlando's Disneyland tomorrow. Please join us?"

"Went there already. Check out Epcot center. Very astonishing."

"Returning shortly. Come along Harold. Fix your own plate."

"Sounds appropriate Al. Humph. Getting hungry."

Monday's red sunrise loomed totally incredible. Snapped five pictures. Drove back to Sand Dune park. Momma was very impressed with their shorter version. 11:00 a.m. Tuesday sponsor placed suitable phone call.

"Hello. Deep sea excursions. Hazel speaking."

"Good morning Hazel. Would like reservations for three adults aboard Joy B. Have anything available?"

"Tomorrow ok? Captain Picket departed already."

"Perfect. Will arrive within 20 minutes with $165 cash. Bye."

"Already plugged small chest freezer in. Works well. Do you want chicken stew with dumplings tonight?"

"Sure darling. Care to take a short ride Dad?"

"Your mother and I plan beach combing. Here. Take this $100 bill."

"No thanks. Angling excursion is on me."

"Look! Been watching that enormous tortoise digging. Presumably making her nest."

"Require assistance chef? Scrubbing vegetables perhaps?"

"Negative Harold. Got everything under control. Enjoy kicking sand."

Tuesday we watched various surfers battling whitecaps. Apparently, a major storm brewed 30 miles east.

Wednesday Momma held down the fort. Although loving ocean views, lighthouses, rolling waves, soaring gulls, she rarely ventures onto boats. Rebukes motion sickness.

"Humph! Simply not worth coping with. Good luck."

Caught nearly 35 pounds of fillets. Froze them.

Thursday Sea World in Orlando overwhelmed us all. Avoiding a major argument I allowed Dad's paying our aquatic excursion. Was astounded mostly by Shamu. (An amiable yet ancient killer whale.) Frolicking antics performed by three airborne dolphins also.

Milled around crystal clear pool Friday. Investigated Japanese sushi restaurant at 3:30. Ordered no food, but truly enjoyed warm bowls of rice wine called sake. Returned to condominium suite. Lightly breaded a large sea trout, then fried him crispy addressing evening's meal.

"Delicious fish. Have done well Pukka."

"Did you employ squid for bait again?"

"Not this time Dad."

"Shrimp. Beached several of these beauties. Both freezers are teeming."

Phone rang.

"Hello."

"Harold?"

"Good evening Grandma. How are things?"

"Can not complain health-wise. Harold there?"

"One minute. Dad? Come here."

"Hi Ma. Any problems?"

"Beverly just left. Enjoyed my meatloaf, baked yams, brown gravy, green beans. She stops by twice daily, mornings and after work. Called Robert. Have no hot water. He said wait an hour for his arrival, but that took place about 3:25."

"Hmm. Probably tripped circuit breaker."

"When coming home?"

"Next week. Late Sunday night though. Will drop by Monday forenoon, May 21st."

"Miss you. Do not get sunstroke. Hey! Bobby's truck just pulled in. Got to run. Will call back after he leaves."

Topped off gas tank Saturday morning and ventured across Tamiami Trail - US route 41. Observed many alligators. Broke out my fly rod. Using weighted streamers I caught five prehistoric gar with awesome teeth, but no bass. Released them all. Smallest post office intrigued Momma. Stopped in Ochopee for late breakfast. My three-egg omelet consisted of sweet sausage, onions, cheese, green peppers. Catfish with eggs for everyone else. Many smoked hams suspended on wire, were visible hanging from the ceiling. Doubled back to route 839, then headed north. Banged right turn onto Alligator Alley. Momma refused to join us on an airboat tour of Lake Okeechobee so we only lingered there long enough to snap pictures. Am sure several bass would have fallen prey, but such is life. Stopped at Publix supermarket. Purchased evaporated plus one gallon fresh milk, butter, potatoes, steaks, whole wheat bread, 12-pack Amstel light bottles. Refilled gas tank at 7-11 convenient store. Drove back to condominium. Prepared moderate-sized kettle of chowder. Broiled rib-eyes. Mashed five Yukon Gold beauties. Heated mixed vegetables. (Microwave oven.) After supper our guests strolled white sandy beach. Carol addressed laundry. (White clothes, sheets, pillowcases.) Then remade beds.

"Almost finished Honey?"

"Nearly. Vacuumed parlor. Scoured bathroom. Disinfected everything. Spraying insect killer as a preventive measure presently."

"Be right back. Visiting upstairs. Suite #4."

Ten minutes later company entered.

"Fill six-pack cooler while darts become pilfered. Departing neighbors demand rematch."

"Annihilated us last episode, but practiced many hours since."

"Checking out before 11:00 tomorrow morning. Difficult believing 14 days fled so quickly."

"Here Pukka. Our mailing address-phone number. Just thought you might enjoy keeping abreast."

"Thanks. Precious card belongs aboard my wallet. Hmm. Safety purposes. Want cold drinks?"

"Corona? If not, brought eight frigid bottles."

"Sorry. Only supplied another brand."

"Run along. Joining proceedings momentarily. Must leave brief message for your parents."

Harold-Althea: Across parking lot. (Recreation Hall with Jim and Marge.) Make yourself comfortable or come join festivities.

*Carol*

Scene ends. Reopens 11:45 a.m. Sunday. May 12th . (Linpav's horse ranch.)

"Absolutely positive about this?"

"Yes Son. Your Dad pronounced. Jack drives us back Thursday afternoon. Plan remaining here until then."

"Enter. Need assistance carting luggage Harold?"

"Only brought these two suitcases. Require no ministration."

"Alright then. Allow my unveiling your sleeping quarters. Follow please."

"Something cooking smells delightful."

"Very appetizing indeed."

"Frying onions, red peppers, garlic. Preparing lamb chops, rice pilaf, hominy grits for lunch."

Made it back to condominium safely. Attended gazebo festivities. Supplied abundant fish chowder.

"Hi Renee. Only seven days remaining. Then vacation ends."

"Heard you have become resident dart champion."

"Beginner's luck. My spouse has been carrying me."

"Delectable soup. Help yourself to foodstuff. Many barbecued items are available."

"Both freezers are full. Be sure to grab their contents next week. Much money involved."

"Sure. Thanks. Hey! Come along. Must introduce your new neighbors. Ben hails from South Carolina. His wife Penny manages an antique store there. Meet designer/draftsman Pukka and his lovely mate Carol. They are Massachusetts residents. Benjamin sells real estate. Plays tennis. Carol works as a certified public accountant. Enjoys golf. Well, must run."

"Construct any architectural blueprints?"

"Yes Ben. Anything/everything mechanical. Large power transformers, municipal water clarification systems, plastic injection molds, package machinery. Care for Amstel light brews?"

"Sounds good."

"Golf intrigues 16 year old son. Has his own clubs."

"Great! Very beneficial exercise. Leave him home?"

"No way. Marc presently visits recreation hall. Free pinball captivates young eyes. Have any children?"

"Must replenish 6-pack cooler. Relapsing soon."

"Sorry Pukka. Feel embarrassed. Ignorant. Sometimes my uneducated mouth can be brutal."

"Hmm. No. Lost our son years ago. God's will."

"That is awful."

"Judging by your tans you have been here awhile. We are only staying one week. Have suggestions on where to site see?"

"Sand dune park. Lovely tropical paradise. Am positive Marc would enjoy Disneyland. Sea world is capacious also. Cape Canaveral was intriguing. Loved Epcot Center, Bush Gardens. Hitting MGM studios tomorrow."

"Arrived by bus this morning. Rented that silver Chevy Eurosport in Gainesville."

"First-class looking car. Ours is the red Plymouth Sundance. We flew down here in April."

"Back again. Hold this Honey, while more chicken wings, potato salad, gherkins become appropriated."

Slid carrying strap up right arm, then over shoulder. Together we all ambled toward food concession. Elected two medium-rare cheeseburgers with onion slices, french fries, Jalapeno peppers. Benjamin enjoyed three bowls of chowder.

"Delicious. Never tasted better. Thick and creamy. Delicious. Could readily manage some Massachusetts restaurant chain."

"Simply followed Grandma's Cookbook. They are all mouth-watering bits of knowledge."

"Obtainable by the general public? Would love purchasing a copy."

"Negative, but plan returning shortly. Do not leave."

15 minutes slid away. Regained my seat.

"Jotted down Grandma's recipe for you."

"Thanks Pukka. Do we owe anything?"

"Of course not. What are neighbors for?"

"Welcome Marc. Glad you could join us."

"Fingers are tired. Put my name up on pinball machine twice. Been playing ping pong with Sally from Idaho. She is only 15 years old, but tough competition."

"Go grab something to eat."

"Ok Dad. Getting hungry."

"Inherited this antique timepiece from my grandfather. Would like having it appraised."

"Hmm. Gold plated. 21 jewels. Not typical railroad variety. Worth about $350. Want to sell this Boker watch right now? Offering $300 cash. Gold chain included."

"No Penny. Thanks for your appraisal though. Value can only increase."

Thursday, pelting rain struck. An hour later everything was dry again. Peeled two large potatoes, then boiled them until nearly cooked. Added five pounds of fish fillets. Continued boiling medley seven more minutes. Drained off water. Three raw eggs. One diced onion. (Medium sized.) Sprinkled 1½ teaspoons dill seed. Pinch of garlic powder. Mangled everything together. Formed (14) 2-inch diameter balls. Let cool adequately. Placed aboard refrigerator. Guests arrived punching 3:30.

"Welcome Althea, Harold."

"Would have been here sooner, but experienced heavy rain."

"Poured here also. Did you lunch?"

"No. Only breakfast. Do not just stand there Harold. Cart those suitcases to our bedroom."

"Ok Al. Returning shortly."

"Marlene attend?"

"Yes. Jack and her both. They presently investigate your delightful swimming pool area."

"Should we join them?"

"Grab 6-pack cooler. Check on things while plates are set out. Dispensing supper at 5:00 o'clock sharp."

"Require helping hands?"

"Unnecessary Momma. Run along, taking Dad with you."

Separately heated spinach, corn, asparagus. Engineered jumbo salad. Turned fry-o-later on. (Highest setting.)

"Honey? Not having any lettuce?"

"Too busy right now. Will have some later. First wave of fish should take about four minutes. Start with these."

"Hmm. Just love delicate asparagus. Want more salad?"

Everyone raved about the main course and for good reason. Tasty. There were no leftovers to contend with.

"Leaving so soon?"

"Affirmative. Must get going. Come along Marlene."

"Thanks again youngest brother. Delicious meal as always. If we do not meet before Massachusetts beckons, enjoy safe flight. Well, see you later."

While my parents explored white sandy beach, Carol loaded dish washer. Perfect time for checking things in Williamstown.

"Hello."

"Hi Grandma. Anything new happening?"

"Just serving supper. Made chipped beef gravy, summer squash, baked Russets. Beverly should arrive fairly soon. Robert corrected hot water problem. Everything works well. Harold available?"

"He is beach walking with Momma right now. Will have him call you later."

"Probably all sun-burnt."

"Not badly. Visited MGM studios last Tuesday. Learned how movies are produced. Very interesting actually. Swarming with many people though."

"Stay alert. Guard your wallet. Many pickpockets thrive amongst those crowded places."

"Always do. Travelers checks are replaceable anyhow."

"Hear something. Hmm. Beverly just pulled in. Enjoy your vacation. Must hang up now. Keep faith."

"Bye."

"Feel like tossing darts?"

"Alright dear. Grab them while Hubby fills 6-pack cooler. Remember to leave same brief note though."

Harold-Althea: We are across parking lot. (Recreation Hall.) Please make yourself comfortable or come join festivities. *Carol*

"Hey Dad. Competition has arrived. Braving our billiard table? Lessons only cost $1."

"Perhaps another time Marc. Came to shoot darts."

"Challenging us as partners? $2 per game."

"Not addressing rookies. Make it $5 apiece each game."

"Done deal Ben."

Time flew. Strolling toward Suite #2 my wife was positively elated.

"Here Honey. Your half. Hmm. $50. Awesome display of marksmanship. Won all six tournaments."

"Thanks. Foolish wager on their part. Tee He. Major blunder for going double or nothing."

"Welcome strangers. Made some popcorn. Want any?"

"Sounds good Althea. Watching anything interesting?"

"Dancing with stars. Weather station predicts no storms."

"Excellent. Dad? Forgot mentioning something. Call Grandma."

"Already did. Around 7:00 o'clock. Shoot billiards tonight?"

"Left our cue sticks home. Tossed darts instead."

Went nowhere Friday. Enjoyed ocean front. Swam in pool. Was hot though. (101 degrees.) Cooked meatloaf, baked potatoes, corn for supper. Investigated Avenue #3 at 5:00 o'clock Saturday. Located Mexican restaurant. Strawberry blonde female bartender appeared thrilled greeting us.

"Welcome to Clancy's Cantina. Observing Cinco de Mayo. $1.00 off on large draft beers."

"Serve Guiness stout on tap?"

"Sorry. Hmm. These handles unveil what we have."

"Ok. Need four glasses of Killian's Irish Red delivered to that table. Kitchen open?"

"Yes. Stacey will serve as your waitress. $8 please."

"Just slip it onto our tab."

Wife ordered Chili Con Queso and Black bean-chicken burrito. Momma elected hamburger plus french fries. Dad favored cheeseburger-onion rings. Jalapeno burger-Cantina Poppers-garden salad with blue cheese for me.

"Honey? What kind of serpent is that?"

"Lamprey eel. Judging by length he must be ancient."

Excellent food. Conceivable price. Friendly atmosphere. Left $15 tip.

7:30 a.m. Sunday while Carol showered I shaved, brewed coffee, removed/stored dishwasher paraphernalia.

"Good morning son. Need any help constructing breakfast?"

"No time for that. Pour yourself some Maxwell House. Employ those Styrofoam cups."

"Lovely bungalow. Ideal location. Best mother's day present ever. Thanks."

"Anytime Momma. Dad up yet?"

"Of course. Who could sleep through all this commotion?"

"Master bathroom is open Althea. Grab this Honey. Bring lengthy silver fishing pole holder. Should have another suitcase prepared soon. Take my key. Oh! Checkbook also."

Silver rod case barely fit into trunk. Slammed red beast closed eventually. Ambled through office entrance.

"Hi. Renee available? Would like saying adios."

"Hey Pukka. I am over here. Next room down."

"Brought both sets of keys as you requested. Paying balance owed."

"Simple enough. $2,400."

"Fantastic late winter retreat. Made several friends. Be sure. Empty both freezers. Much money is involved."

"Will do. Probably within 90 minutes. Enjoy a safe flight. Bring your relatives anytime. Cool family."

"Well, business stands complete. Was pleasurable making your acquaintance. So long."

"Wait. Take my card. Wrote pertinent home phone number down on backside. Usually available at one or the other. Humph. Why are all good ones always taken?"

"Bye Renee."

Loaded Plymouth Sundance approaching maximum capacity. Headed north. Accomplished Daytona. Stopped addressing fuel gauge level. Ate breakfast at Friendly's. Returned rental vehicle. Took shuttle bus. Left airport. Arrived in Albany wearing tank top, sandals and shorts. Wow! Only 43 degrees. Freezing. Waiting for portage, my brother showed up.

"Welcome back. Been out in sunlight obviously. Enjoy your extended getaway?"

"Super vacation. What was wrong with our hot water?"

"Nothing serious Dad. Circuit breaker tripped. That Lincoln Continental of yours is extremely powerful. Got here way ahead of schedule."

"Best not be speeding with my wheels."

"Hey! Here comes our stuff. Capture silver tube Pukka. Grab blue suitcase Carol."

Scene ends. Reopens Tuesday May 28th at 5:40.

"Welcome home darling. Guess what? Never mind. Our vacation pictures arrived in today's mail."

"Great! Been preparing supper obviously."

"Nothing special. We are visiting Grandma tonight."

"Unannounced?"

"Of course not. Already substantiated everything. Told her expect our 6:00 o'clock arrival. Mom and Dad are going to be there."

French onion soup recipe.
¾ stick unsalted butter
2½ tablespoons olive oil
Three red & four sizeable sweet onions (Sliced thin.¼ inch thick or less.)
One quart each: chicken & beef broth
1½ teaspoons: parsley flakes, crushed bay leaves, dried thyme
One tablespoon wine vinegar
Three ounces Worcestershire sauce
Five slices toasted French bread (2" thick.)
Five slices Swiss cheese
¾ cup each: grated Parmesan, shredded Mozzarella
1¼ teaspoon each: black pepper, paprika

Melt butter-olive oil in large stock pot. Add onions. Caramelize on medium-high setting 40 minutes. (Stirring frequently.) Introduce Worcestershire, broth, parsley, bay leaves, thyme. Continue high-simmering 20 minutes. Decrease temperature (Medium-low.) Add vinegar-pepper. Stir thoroughly. Cover. Arrange five oven-proof crocks aboard baking sheet. Fill each 60% full, then top-off with toasted bread, Swiss, parmesan, Mozzarella. Lace heavily with sprinkled paprika. Let rest. When ready to serve broil uncovered six minutes.

"Hi everyone. Pukka will join proceedings momentarily."

"Come here Carol. Look at these pictures of our Florida excursion."

"Sure thing Althea. Brought many ourselves.

# Accidental death

Grandma's Veal Oscar recipe: 5 lbs live lobster, 1 gallon Chianti wine, 6 cloves fresh garlic, ¼ pound stick of unsalted butter, one cup milk, ½ lb each: shredded Gruyere, cheddar cheese, 2 lbs veal cutlets, ¾ cup flour, 20 spears blanched asparagus. In steamer's base: Chianti-garlic. Using heavy instrument (Cleaver or heavy spoon.) Crack lobster's shell (Claws and tails.) Place aboard steamer's upper section. Steam on high until shells turn red. (12 or 15 minutes.) Once cooled enough remove meat to place into base unit along with wine-garlic medley.

Prepare delicate sauce: Melt 60% of butter in large saucepan (Medium-low setting.) Stir in milk. Cook three minutes. Gradually whisk in both cheese portions. Once fully melted and lump-free, cover. Remove from heat.

Using the remaining butter, fry veal. (Breaded.) 1½ minutes per side. Plate cutlets. Bury with lobster chunks. Deposit asparagus. Lace everything with delicate sauce. Serve immediately.

Dear Jim - Marge Feustel;

Another month has slipped by. Everyone here is happy and healthy. Carol says HI. She has not arrived home from work yet, but is due any minute. Located your mailing address this morning while searching my wallet. Have not played darts recently. Or golf either. Actually, poor Pukka is job searching presently. The corporation for whom I was employed closed down. That situation involves comprehension time. Went for a job interview last Wednesday. Awful shame. If the opening becomes mine, must travel 140 miles per day. Short term position. Was told six months or less. Well, hear wife's car. Must sign off now.

Your friend; Pukka Carpenter

"Welcome home darling."

"Thanks Honey. Boiling something?"

"Good guess. Picked three supermarket bags full of dandelions. Exercising our latest acquisition presently. Added much freshened salt pork plus two onions, six whole redskin potatoes and ten of Norman's hot dogs weighing over 1¼ lbs."

"Sounds wonderful. They are perhaps my favorite green vegetable. We get any urgent mail today?"

"Nothing important. Just composed this brief message. Will require one of our stamps."

"Parlor desk. Top drawer. Must have bunches left. Did you receive first unemployment check finally?"

"Yes. Plan cashing it tomorrow."

"How much will you be depositing each week?"

"Unsure still. Probably $330. Possibly $350."

"Where headed now?"

"Calling favorite neighbors. Momma can set out plates and silverware."

Scene ends. Reopens in Grandma's apartment 55 minutes later.

"Good evening everyone. Supplied ample dandelion greens, several jumbo hot dogs also."

"True folks. Look! Largest rectangular pan we have. Heavy gauge. Eight inches deep. Covers two burners."

"Wow! Am totally overwhelmed. Where did my grandson ever find such an impressive cooking utensil?"

"Stainless steel hey?"

"Restaurant Supply store in Pittsfield. Yes, Ma. Should last through many blistering encounters. Cost enough. $119 plus tax. Hmm. Setting this on your electric range. Extremely gravitational. Must weigh over 20 pounds."

"Grab serving apparatus Al. You know where they reside. Require two large forks and perhaps a large scoop."

"Any luck searching for work yet?"

"Nothing close to our area. Might be forced to job shop. East Windsor, Connecticut or possibly Delmar, NY."

"Must be joking. Talking logic Son. They are hiring drivers at Greenburg's. Switch professions temporarily."

"Applied there last Tuesday. Had an interview, but failed."

"Seems absurd. Reason being?"

"Was asked why I was considering such a major pay loss. What would happen should another design position become available. Apparently, they only seek less qualified employees."

"Seems absurd."

"Terrible shame. Penalized for being honest. Saw this ad in today's Berkshire Eagle newspaper. Check it out."

Help wanted: Seeking designer/draftsman. Cadra-Versacad proficient. Geometric dimensioning-tolerancing knowledge required. Only experienced strongly motivated individuals need apply. Supply resume. Address…

"Wonderful! We could utilize one vehicle. Surely Hubby mitigates possessing over 17 years of education."

September 4, 1991. Went for job interview. Successfully landed position. Wife came home on schedule.

"How did things progress?"

"Excellent. Officially rejoining our labor force."

"Great! Starting when?"

"Two weeks from now. Working as primary assistant to head engineer of research and development."

"Whew! Knew everything would materialize."

"Should prove interesting. Did not prepare anything. We dine in some fine restaurant tonight."

"Salaried or hourly assignments?"

"My option. Undecided still. Either way awesome income involved. Leaning toward punching a clock. Get paid extra for overtime that way. $37.50 per hour."

Scene ends. Reopens Monday September 16 at 5:35 p.m.

"Welcome home. Just arrived myself ten minutes ago. How did first day transpire?"

"Totally impressed. Met several people. Am working in enormous mansion. Brought this extra large pizza."

"Hmm. Set out plates. Phone rang, but no one answered. Oh! There it goes again. Be right back."

Five minutes later.

"Who was that?"

"Grandma. Told her we will be there shortly."

Soon we sat at Grandma's table.

"Called Althea. She is bringing red-skin potato salad. Already set out five plates. So... Enjoy your new job?"

"Very much. Surrounded by brilliant engineers. Have a small office right now."

"Good cracker. Hey! Best address garage door. Surely your parents."

"Hi Pukka."

"Hello Ma. Dad."

"Good evening everyone."

"Need any help carrying things?"

"Grab this hefty Tupperware bowl please. Harold? Set those items on kitchen counter."

"Find out labor responsibilities yet?"

"Their current patent expires in two years. Conducting major redesign incorporating several improvements so Sparkling Waters can apply for another."

"Awesome! Guaranteed 24 month employment."

"Was interviewed by Henry Mason, my immediate supervisor. His grandfather is corporation president."

"Establish any time schedule?"

"Unlimited overtime. Includes weekends. Must be there between 9:00 and 3:00 o'clock Monday thru Friday."

"Have access to a telephone in case of emergencies?"

"Naturally darling. Got one on my desk. Local number. Simply call main office requesting extension #307."

"Holidays paid?"

"Yes. 14 per year. Many benefits. 401K retirement plan. Health Insurance. Wife included. Full dental. Five sick days. 10 personal. $1,000 Christmas bonus. Only one week vacation initially, but three next year."

"Wow! My son has made the grade. Proud of you Pukka."

"Wife too Honey. Guess we will not worry about overdue bills anymore."

"Serve your redskin potato salad Al. Getting hungry."

"Allow me. Start with pizza Harold."

"Hmm. Looks scrumptious. Pepperoni, sausage, mushrooms, cheese, onion."

"Never cared for fungus personally."

"They are super. No problem Ma. Sort through and pick them off. All the more for me. These magnificent beauties must be Portabellas."

"Slide your plate closer Harold."

Dear Benjamin - Penny Simpson;

Florence Carpenter is no longer with us. Police report verifies her death was accidental. They are not planning further investigations. Case closed. She was an unbelievable influence to all. Dad harvests everything well.

On lighter note, we remain healthy. Feel as though Grandma was let down. There remains unfinished business, but am not at liberty exposing private deals. Knew something was awry though. Ordinarily her departing words were 'Keep Faith'. Notoriously. Instead, she babbled 'See you on the other side.' Ouch! Should have guessed. Awesome woman. Have not heard from our South Carolina friends yet, but hope we will soon. Carol says 'Hi'.

Pukka Carpenter

Hello Massachusetts buddies:

Sorry. Woeful recent loss. Please rest assured 'God works in mysterious ways.' Ready? Selling that 21 jewel Boker watch plus gold chain? Discussed issues with Ben. Offering $700 cash. Pewter watch fobs are plentiful. Hardly interested concerning anything pewter.

*Penny Simpson*

Tuesday November 19 at 11:15 a.m. Immediate supervisor, Henry Mason, entered my office. Not alone. Was introduced. Karmen, an attractive blond female, corporation's vice president. They were both eager to view exactly what newly designed version looked like. They viewed renovated, totally unique idea on their 21 inch monitor. Everything tranquilized reasonable. Explained innovative theories. Henry was sold on novel idea, but male opinion mattered little. Vice president shook her head, then merely wandered away.

Wednesday morning punched in before 7:00 o'clock. By 7:25 walked into unfamiliar machine shop.

"Looking for Greg Zimmerman. Correct?"

"Exactly."

"Congratulations. Found me. Called yesterday afternoon?"

"Yes. My name is Pukka. Am working for Sparkling Waters as a designer/draftsman specialist."

"Alright then. Brought your blueprints obviously."

"Right again. Even supplied this three-dimensional computer disc. Select your total price?"

"Told you already. Must tool up for this single item. Very expensive maneuver. Sure about quantity? Just require one?"

"Merely producing a chancy prototype. If my design works we will definitely need many others only larger."

"Hmm. Talking three days labor. Expensive stainless steel components. Might fail anyway."

"Never mind. Will need my blueprints returned along with AutoCAD disc. Waste of time stopping here."

"Slow down. Had best be a jumbo sucker. $600 total. Half up front. Carrying $300 cash down payment?"

Punched out 12:01. Grabbed corned beef sandwich. Explored lower mansion's periphery. Wow! Junkyard of discarded quality items. Veritable goldmine. Several interesting attractions. Tires, stainless steel plates, tanks, bars, tubing, pipes, angles, shafts. Made it back to log in 12:29. Climbed 16 stairs leading to Henry's office.

"Hey boss. Very busy right now?"

"Awaiting an important incoming message. Any problem?"

"Was browsing during lunchtime. Spotted ten-foot long galvanized horse trough behind lower mansion. Can it be used for research projects? Could prove useful."

"Foresee little problems. Tell Jim Whittick 'Haul that reservoir inside'. You have an authority over everyone down there. Keep the crew in our fabrication shop occupied. They are all hourly employees. Glad you stopped. Show me how to extrude flat surfaces in AutoCAD."

"Simple feat actually. Allow me to sit there a minute. Watch as this entire medley becomes highlighted. Next, activate drop-down menu. Labeled Sol-extrude, select…"

Phone rings.

"Why now? Take your seat back. Will explain fully another time."

Ring.

"Thanks. Think perhaps waiting until later would prove beneficial."

Ring.

"Lenox Sparkling Waters. Henry Mason speaking. Good afternoon Karmen. Have been waiting patiently for your answer. Ok. See you soon."

Friday November 22 arrived home.

"Just checked. No mail today?"

"Apparently not. Want turkey reheated again for supper?"

"Kidding? Two consecutive days? Microwave TV dinners instead. Fish or something. Working tomorrow?"

"Only until noon. Why?"

"Stop by. Meet me at the upper mansion. Would enjoy displaying my office."

"Should I bring something for lunch?"

"Good plan darling."

Saturday: Punched in at 8:35. Ambled downhill to lower mansion. Spotted shop manager, Mr. Whittick.

"Hi Jim. Mount those brackets yet? Not sure, but think we will need everything prepared by Tuesday."

"Come see for yourself. Finished implementing your blueprints yesterday afternoon."

Moments later while I inspected his handiwork,

"Looks exactly like your illustration. Right? Even installed variable speed motor as specified."

"Have done well. Not finished yet though. Require waterproof baffle on far end."

"Can not weld galvanized steel. Have pressure treated plywood ½ inch thick."

"That will suffice. Employ silicone caulk. After it dries, nearly fill this end with water."

"Where exactly does this baffle get installed?"

"Here. Cut both edges of plywood at 45 degree angles. Slip into tank's curvature."

"How high above surface seems appropriate? One inch?"

"Hmm. Works for me. Leaving now. Have fun."

Carol arrived shortly after 1:00 o'clock. Receptionist directed her accurately.

"Thought you said your workplace was small."

"Hi darling. Please be seated in my visitor's chair. Be right back. Must punch out."

Returned within five minutes.

"Back again. What kind of pizza did you deliver?"

"Sausage, onion and yellow banana peppers. Brought paper plates. Lemon-lime soda also. That device have any name?"

"Called a plotter. Produces D-sized or smaller blueprints. Want to observe it in action?"

"Not now. Another time perhaps. Find out anything yet? Does your theory work?"

"Will know more Tuesday. Excellent pizza."

# Slovenian Jig

Sunday after church Carol broiled two jumbo hamburgers, then served them with mashed potatoes, brown mushroom gravy. Supper was absolutely delicious. Told her so. After dining she appeared inquisitive.

"What are you cooking now?"

"Frying hot sausage. Boiling flat pasta. Preparing tomorrow evening's lasagna meal."

"Thanks Honey. Hmm. That explains things, including these additional ingredients."

Alternately layered tomatoes, drained bulk hot sausage, pre-cooked pasta, cubed raw onion, Ricotta cheese. Four installments filled casserole dish.

"Microwave oven empty? This medley must cool adequately somewhere safe before hitting refrigerator."

"Yes. Well probably. Tell me more about your latest project. Hubby seems worried."

"Not at liberty to broadcast details. They dispense first prototype late morning. Cost $800 altogether."

"Spent $800 without informing me?"

"No dear. Sparkling Waters fronted all necessary cash. $600 plus $200 for mounting brackets- labor. Could get severely fired should the three-bladed scoop flunk."

"Stop fretting. Grandma would say 'Keep faith'. Even if that particular redesign somehow fails, we still have each other. Surely, it will perform splendidly."

Monday November 22 at 11:35 Greg Zimmerman accompanied by two of his employees delivered unique design to lower mansion as directed. By 3:15 everything including the drive chain was installed. Mr. Whittick cranked up tiny electric propulsion motor.

"Hey Jim. Rotating too fast. Decrease speed."

"That better? Lowest setting. Can not adjust rotation any slower."

"Perfect!"

"How do we test this beast? Have no wood chips available."

"Styrofoam packaging peanuts float. Should prove worthy. Brought an entire trash bag full. Depositing them now."

Instead of dumping in customary fashion, collected peanuts entered central tube where they rushed forward.

"Unbelievable! Eliminates exit trough's purpose entirely. Major cost saving."

"Whew! Complete success."

Punched out at 4:40. Drove home. Placed relevant phone call.

"Hello. Althea speaking."

"Good evening Ma. Who plowed our driveway?"

"Robert just left. Carol available?"

"She has yet to arrive. Make any supper plans?"

"Barbecuing spareribs. Defrosted several. At least eight. Come join festivities. Structured some blackberry pies. Harold enjoys them."

"Will be there before 6:00 with baked lasagna. Mortgage payment also. Bye."

Scene ends. Reopens at 5:55 as Carol pushes garage's smaller side door open.

"Welcome strangers. Notice anything different?"

"Someone has been stacking firewood."

"Right. Four cord. Set that casserole dish aboard our wood stove. Already placed spareribs inside of it five minutes ago. That's why door remains ajar. We dine out here tonight. Bring my check?"

"Count this cash. Should be simple enough. All $100 bills."

"Grab seats. Start with salad. Returning shortly with your receipt."

"Hi Dad. Where should we sit?"

"Matters little. Al occupies this spot next to me though."

"Chunky blue cheese or zesty Italian dressing?"

"Blue cheese as usual."

"Should have known."

"Here son. Signed, sealed, delivered."

"Welcome back. Thanks Ma."

"Whew! Must be over 80 degrees out here. Serving main course immediately, then shutting blistering inferno nearly off. Come along Al. Bequeath lasagna."

Supper tasted excellent. Great salad. Delicious spareribs.

"Anyone care for more blackberry pie?"

"Maybe another thin sliver."

"One slice was plenty. Not excessively sweet. My Hubby does not know what he has missed."

"We are renting Grandma's apartment these days. Single girl. Non-smoker. Teaches kindergarten children."

"Additional income always comes in handy. Tell Harold about your latest design? Would like hearing about that endeavor myself."

"Some other time perhaps. Need assistance washing dishes?"

"Certainly. Can help by rinsing plates."

15 minutes later Momma engaged their dishwasher.

"Nothing interesting on TV yet. Shall we play Polish pitch? House residents versus welcomed guests."

"Sure. Only 7:15 currently. Have not burlesqued cards. Humph. Been ages."

"Grab our plastic deck, while I install fresh batteries aboard automatic shuffler. Bid high."

By 9:20 my parents had ingested much information concerning municipal water clarification practices. Carol announced last game.

"Since scoop design stands completed, will my son be getting laid off again soon?"

"Seems unlikely. Working on three other projects simultaneously."

"Resonates as foolishness to these old ears. Spreading yourself excessively thin. Conquer one goal at a time."

"Makes perfect sense. Much truth has spoken there. But then again, Pukka multi-tasks very well. Always did."

Monday December 2. Punched clock 8:39. Doodled on scratch pad until 10:50. Someone tapped lightly.

"Please enter. Hi boss."

"Good morning. Just walked back up here. Been down lower mansion. The theory works. Grandpa actually danced a Slovenian jig while babbling some foreign language. He speaks five of them fluently, but suffers communication problems addressing English occasionally. Especially when he gets excited."

"Must have very high intelligence Henry."

"Oh yes. Getting old now. Humph. Still very sharp. They presently scheme to short shot Christmas bonuses claiming Pukka has not been here long enough."

"They reconsidering that detrimental action?"

"Possibly. If latest bill passes through Board of Directors. Guarantees void. What updates planning next?"

"Come closer. Investigate these sketches of bottom sand scraper."

"Explain what these diminutive lines represent."

"Continuous hinge running full length."

"Poor theory. Excessively expensive. Rubber bends naturally anyway. Require no additional hinging effect."

"Reached exactly same conclusion. Observe rendering #2."

"Much better idea. Remember now, we only deal with all stainless steel construction. Surely, steel would damage its mating material. Unless of course. Oh, never mind. Grinding full radius would be cost prohibitive."

"This integral depiction addresses all these issues. Sound design. Might tweak things slightly. Require 12 hours. Should have a primary archetypal drawn up on computer by noontime tomorrow. Drop back after lunch."

"Heading home soon. Usually do. Less than one quarter mile jaunt. Grilling extra lean hamburgers. Please join festivities."

"Maybe later next week. Supplied two hefty turkey sandwiches with mayonnaise. Hate wasting food."

"Only five seats on our executive Board of Directors. Grandpa retains one as does Karmen. Definitely the odds are favorable."

"Hmm. 40% chance. Thanks for additional information."

"Bye."

"Drive safely."

"Always do. Replacing vehicles can grow very expensive."

Punched out 12:01. Ate both sandwiches. Worried myself sick. 60% against. Raw deal. Arrived home 5:35. Investigated mailbox. Proceeded up driveway. Parked beside Carol's Volkswagen Golf. Climbed front stairway. Smelled onions frying. Threw door open.

"Welcome back. Froze all remaining turkey leftovers. Enjoying beef liver, boiled potatoes, cabbage for supper."

"Yummy. Baked too big a turkey for Thanksgiving. Picked up our mail."

"Anything interesting?"

"Gas bill, Williamstown supermarket flyer, one letter. Nothing else."

"Seem depressed. Bad day at work?

"Probably losing $1,000 Christmas bonus."

"Can they do that?"

"Unsure. Guess so."

"Damn. They lied. Offer any explanation?"

"Am considered a 'New employee', lacking adequate service longevity."

"Supper will be served in five minutes. Set out two plates. Silverware also."

Scene ends. Reopens 1:05 Tuesday December 3. Immediate supervisor enters my office hauling a compact white refrigerator.

"Thought you might find use of this cooler. Possess two. Operates well."

"Thanks Henry. Leave door open. Plug donation in somewhere over there."

Three minutes later.

"Making significant progress?"

"Plotted out renovated concept. Look for yourself. Blueprints reside on that table. Be there shortly. Putting my lunch leftovers into recent contribution."

"Love your proposal. Makes perfect sense. Simplifies manufacturing. Actually, foresee many advantages."

"Already called around requesting estimates. Might take several days to receive all price quotes."

"Incorporate these new design modifications immediately. Tell Jim Whittick we need four sections ASAP."

"Could end costing more."

"One 15 degree bend. Eight ¾ inch holes. Break sharp edges. Humph. Not discussing much money here."

"Theory remains untested. Represents poor engineering practice."

"Only ordered four sections for test purposes. If everything passes, look at the advantages. Unique system is ingenious. Can not possibly fail. Will prove that fact next week."

Accomplished nine minute trek. Entered lower mansion's machine shop area. Was greeted shortly.

"Hi Pukka. Sorry. Did not see you. Was busy welding. Wait long?"

"No Jim. Just got here. Brought another schematic."

"More horse trough refinements?"

"Been toying with various innovations. Yes. Making several horse trough changes. Not today though. Instead, take a glance at this detailed drawing."

Musing B-sized sheet, Mr. Whittick removed welding helmet, shook his head, glanced down at cement floor.

"Can not bend 5/8 inch thick stainless steel 5-foot long. Our brake only has 40-inch capacity."

"Ok with drilling all ¾ inch holes?"

"Naturally. No problem there. Drawing states quantity=4. That accurate?"

"Yes. 32 holes altogether."

"Hmm. Probably want this done yesterday as usual."

"Eight days maximum time limit. Sooner would be best."

"Total price: $1,960."

"Sounds fair. Pay attention to my handiwork. Everything must pass inspection. Break all sharp edges, plus .06 radius one specified edge."

"Stop down Tuesday morning for current status report."

"Ball is in your glove. Do not drop it."

Walked back to upper mansion. Doodled until 5:30. Punched out. Drove home. Investigated empty mailbox.

"Hi. Have been expecting you. Stop somewhere, or bag some overtime?"

"Was involved with work projects. How did your day go?"

"Better now. Want hot dogs for supper?"

"Yes dear, with spicy hot chili. No mail today?"

"Guess not. Never opened yesterday's letter. Still resides on parlor's desk."

Dear Pukka & Carol Carpenter:

Bearing good news. New Smyrna Beach wants you back this spring. We only increased our prices $150 per week. Come renew your suntans situated at ocean side. Act fast.

Renee Letourneau

Ps: Thanks for all the fish, frozen veggies, steaks, etc.

# Christmas Bonus

Tuesday December 10 punched time clock 7:29. Gathered up paperwork. Walked downhill. Only one vehicle resided in parking lot. Entered lower mansion's ground floor fabrication shop.

"Hi Pukka. Awfully early. Care for coffee?"

"Sounds good Jim. Black. No sugar."

Minutes later, could hear trucks arriving outdoors. Mr. Whittick advanced closer while holding green cup.

"Might be hot. Best wait until it cools."

"Not in any particular rush."

"Ordered those plates. Subcontracted 15 degree bending process. Probably start drilling holes tomorrow."

"Have another similar project. Investigate this proposal."

He studied my blueprint. Designer sipped green holder's steaming content.

"Well? Can you install 5/8 inch projection welded studs?"

"Stainless steel like the plates?"

"Exactly."

"Where is unit located?"

"Guessing maybe 15 yards. That 20 foot long specimen."

".06 radius. 32 studs times $26 each. Hmm. $802."

"Humph. Slight miscalculation there buddy. $832."

"Ok then. Thanks. $832.

"Done deal. When starting?"

"Maybe this afternoon. Depends on required 1/3 of total price down payment."

"No problem. Setting your cup here. Coffee was not bad. Bye."

Scene ends. Reopens 5:35. Recognized familiar engine noise ascending our driveway. Continued unloading dishwasher, then stacking plates. Door opens.

"Welcome home."

"Thanks Honey. Surprised me being here already."

"Managed half hour overtime."

"Volkswagen needs replacement serpentine belt. Man at Jason's garage informs it is cracked in several places."

"Get any price estimate?"

"$20 for parts."

"Buy one. I will install lengthy serpentine beauty myself. Beats paying $60 per hour labor."

"Seems unlikely, lacking appropriate tools."

"Only require long-handled breaker bar and 1½ inch socket. Elementary task will not consume more than five minutes."

"Great! Who cooks supper tonight?"

"You can. Simply microwave Thanksgiving leftovers. Must use them up before they become freezer-burnt."

"Hear any more news about your promised $1.000 bonus?"

"Nothing yet. Waiting still. Should receive at least $200. Possibly $250. Working the day before Christmas?"

"No. Why ask?"

"Sparkling Waters sponsors their holiday pizza festival. Abundant unrestricted cold beer will be supplied."

"Hmm. Free beer. Hubby apparently requisitions a sober designated driver."

"Wife gets to meet my fellow subordinates. Party begins at high noon. What do you say?"

"We leave before 5:00 o'clock. Hate driving with blaring oncoming headlights. Any mail today?"

"Nothing earthshaking. Positioned everything on parlor's couch."

"Investigating immediately."

As requested, we are reminding you that it is time for your dental cleaning and oral cancer exam. Please call if the scheduled time is not convenient. Thursday afternoon January 2 @ 2:00 o'clock.

"Whew! Somehow six months has elapsed."

"You never use additional sugar. Teeth are perfect. Keep them that way."

Wednesday morning December 11 immediate supervisor entered my office at 10:47.

"Just left main office. Confirmed your $278 withdrawal. Was merely wondering where you spent the cash."

"Jim Whittick needed down payment money to implement bottom scraper's mating surface. Wrong?"

"Good job. Drop everything. Have another assignment. Grandfather flies to Europe Saturday allotting little time for this rush venture. He wants to submit a $900,000 proposal. Brought several photographs. Placing them over here on your other desk."

Thursday heavy snow plummeted all afternoon. Punched out 5:32. Cautiously drove home. Executed u-turn. Backed partly up driveway. Parked directly beside wife's car. Walked through six inches of white stuff.

"Welcome back. Not fussing with supper tonight. Clam chowder, hamburgers."

"Sounds delicious."

"Grabbed our mail."

"Saw telltale footprints. Buy your serpentine belt today?"

"Yes. Cost $21.17 including tax. Left it on my car's back seat."

"Heading next door. Telling Dad we need tools for 15 minutes."

"Eating at 7:00. Please hurry. Hmm. Could make potato salad."

"Unnecessary dear. Bye."

Redressed within 35 minutes.

"Back already?"

"Obviously. Simple affair. Storm has run its course. Not snowing anymore."

"Great! Know something? Jason's Garage would have charged $60 minimum. Thanks Honey."

Friday 3:15 Henry knocked, then gained admittance to my office.

"Grandpa altered his flight schedule. Departing for Bradley International airport immediately."

"Perfect timing. Job stands complete. Here are the blueprints. Run along and catch him before he leaves."

20 minute later Henry returned smiling.

"Mission accomplished. Have done well."

Tuesday December 24 12:47 Pizza party was in full swing. Performed ample introductions. Karmen strolled halfway downstairs wearing silver-green evening gown. Stopped long enough to welcome everyone, lingeringly descended remaining stairs carrying tan briefcase.

"She looks beautiful."

"Yes dear. Be right back. Confiscating another ice cold Heineken. How is that Pepsi holding out?"

"Fine for now."

Left gathering at 4:40. Wife drove.

"Enjoy yourself? Drank several free beers."

"Immensely. Pull over."

"Drunk? Feeling sick?"

"Negative. Just investigative."

Carol located rest area. Stopped.

"Curious about what?"

"My Christmas bonus check."

"Well? Get the full amount? Honey? Say something."

# Reincarnation

Thursday January 2 punched out 1:02. Drove to dentist's new location. Debarked at 1:45. Announced my presence. Sat in waiting room 10 minutes. Flipped through Outdoor Life magazine. Woman approached. Her nametag read 'Elizabeth'.

"Mr. Carpenter?"

"Yes miss ah."

"Lisa. Follow me please."

After accomplishing panoramic x-rays she led to another room.

"Please be seated. Comfortable?"

"Very."

"The doctor presently examines your x-rays. He will be here shortly."

15 minutes later Dr. Barlett arrived. Offered his hand. We shook.

"Hi Warren. Everything look alright?"

"Concerned actually. Been having any dental problems lately?"

"Nothing extraordinary. Why?"

"Surprising response. You suffer a cracked tooth that requires immediate attention. Still employed with electric corporation? Insured?"

"They folded up. Working in Lenox these days. Have another insurance policy through Sparkling Waters."

"Excellent. Will schedule a follow-up appointment within two weeks. Crowns cost $980. Did you change your profession?"

"No. Just designing different items."

"Only have high praises for Sparkling Waters. Always contended with silt in our water before. Not these days. No residue at the bottom of my bathtub. Been employed there long?"

"Four months thus far."

3:55 Warren handed me complimentary bag containing toothbrush and toothpaste, then escorted patient to receptionist area.

"Bye Pukka. See you January 16. Floss daily. Good luck with awesome new job."

Wife arrived home at 5:30.

"Hi Honey. Been here awhile?"

"Yes dear. Over an hour. Dentist appointment lasted longer than expected. Dr. Barlett installed a temporary molar tooth."

"Something cooking smells delicious."

"Beef stroganoff. Not ready yet though."

"Humph. Ridiculous. Still amazed. Who would have thought?"

"Beef stroganoff?"

"No silly. Hubby received a $5,000 Christmas bonus. Whew! Proud of you."

Friday 11:35 immediate supervisor knocked on my office door.

"Please enter."

"Good morning. Interrupting anything?"

"Working out polymorphic details. Been toying with another design perception. Investigate those schematics on my other desk."

Henry studied pertinent blueprints for 10 minutes in silence.

"What thinking? Baffled tank would eliminate all those thick-walled pipes."

"Brilliant concept. When might detail drawings become available?"

"40 days. Possibly less. Already finalized raw water's 6" x 9" rectangular distribution orifice."

"Rectangular? Think that theory might work?"

"Probably. Think so. Simple design actually. Fully adjustable from outside the unit."

"Great idea! Where are you headed?"

"Hitting time clock."

"Grilling hot sausages on gas grill. Come hop in my Suzuki."

"Hmm. Beats peanut butter sandwiches. Ok."

Moments later seated aboard a lounge chair situated on Henry's raised deck.

"Two patties enough?"

"Flawless."

"Should they start burning, flip them over."

Soon, Henry returned with a 6-pack cooler."

"Here. Help yourself. Ever play paintball?"

"Michelob Ultra?"

"Only imprisons 2.6 grams of carbohydrates per can."

"Yummy. Low carbohydrate diets are best. Never indulged with paintball guns."

"Much fun. 34 members comprise our group. Usually we divide forces into six unequal squads."

"Ever win?"

"Of course. Well, sometimes. Buns are toasted perfectly. Have another cold one. Lunch is served."

Punched clock 12:57. Loaded C-sized sheet of paper, then sent latest design to plotter. Various colored pens danced awhile. Conducted downhill trek. Located Mr. Whittick.

"Hi Jim. Brought some more horse trough alterations. Would enjoy their immediate amalgamation."

"No can do. Segmented bottom scraper functions admirably. Surprised everyone."

"Any large water pumps available?"

"How big?"

"Three horsepower."

"Hold on. Must contemplate. Hmm. Have an ancient one. Malfunctions now. Could order another. List price is over $4,000."

"Where might this broken prototype be viewed?"

"Unsure. Could check the old mushroom house."

"Door locked?"

"Not during business hours."

"Currently busy hey?"

"Got that right."

"For how long?"

"Four weeks behind. Try again mid-February."

Located point of interest. Jotted down all pertinent information. Walked back to office. Placed phone calls.

"Hi darling. Am working until 6:00. See you about 6:30. Start supper."

"Gould corporation. Beatrice speaking."

"Good afternoon. Would like price quote for refurbishing one of your products."

"Serial number?"

Scene ends. Reopens 6:35 as wife welcomes me home.

"Got your message. Thanks. Hot dogs boiled forever, but have not split open. Also baking cheese-macaroni."

"Sounds terrific. Love Norman's jumbo wieners."

"More than Carol?"

"Come give me a hug. Been hectic chaos all day."

Hug plus bonus kiss.

"Sorry about the poor lunch."

"Superb cuisine. Lengthy story. Hot dogs are done. Let's eat."

Carol shook her head.

"Spent nearly $1,250 of company's money? Scary stuff."

"Was necessary. Humph. Over $300 went for shipping. Am positive Henry will approve this employee's logical actions."

"Raised deck hey? His house nice?"

"Beautiful ranch-style building surrounded by wildlife sanctuary where paintball games are officiated."

10:15 a.m. Wednesday January 16, 2002 Dr. Warren Barlett replaced temporary molar with permanent tooth. Dental insurance paid all but $196. Wrote out check. Returned to office 12:57. Phone rang shortly thereafter.

"Sparkling Waters. Engineering department."

"Hi Pukka. Jim whittick calling. Gould delivered rebuilt water pump today. Awaiting further instructions."

"Afternoon Jim. Be right there."

Gathered C-sized blueprint, parts list. Accomplished short downhill walk. Delivered paperwork. Waited.

"Any questions?"

"No. Crystal clear details speak for themselves. May require three more silicone caulk tubes. Have everything else."

"How many hours labor?"

"20. Should have horse trough modified and pump installed by Thursday noontime."

"Total price?"

"$495. Discounting possible overtime."

"Done deal. Will personally drop your $165 down payment off early Tuesday morning. Take care."

Immediate supervisor dropped in 3:15.

"Stopped by at 11:00, but you had punched out."

"My dentist rectified a major cracked tooth problem."

"Parboiling drumsticks tonight. Do not bring peanut butter sandwiches tomorrow. Gas grill hungers another workout. Like barbecued chicken?"

"Sure. Invitation accepted. Expended $1,247 repairing company's broken water pump."

"Good job. New models sell for $4,000 plus. Testing your latest design anytime soon?"

"Yes. Wednesday or Thursday."

"Super. Eliminating all those expensive bent pipes would result in a colossal savings."

"Hitting main office up for more research dollars Tuesday. Ok?"

"Use your own judgement. Located this interesting catalogue. Check out the economical sand separator prices. Our current enormous model costs slightly over $42,000."

"Will do."

"Well, expecting an important client. Wish me luck. Got to run. Remember. Lunch at my place tomorrow."

"Thanks for informative catalogue. Good luck Henry. Bye."

Arrived home 6:04.

"Mouth is probably sore. Mashed potatoes. Broiling hamburgers with brown gravy addressing supper."

"Unnecessary precaution. Never felt better. Famished."

"Eat anything today?"

"Too busy. Oh! Boss invited me over his place for lunch tomorrow. Serving barbecued chicken legs."

"Be attentive. He might prefer friendly male companionship over women. Get my drift?"

"Wrong darling. Henry was engaged several months. His fiancé died in a mysterious car crash. Just one lonely guy. Highly intelligent engineer."

"Merely lecturing remain cautious."

"Enough said anatomizing that topic."

"Left before 5:30. Labor eight hours?"

"Exactly. 6:00 to 9:30 and 1:00 until 5:30."

"Long weekend coming up. Make any plans?"

"Oh! Martin Luther King day. Totally slipped my mind. He was a great man. Hmm. Perhaps we could enjoy a brief vacation someplace nearby. Best pack our suitcases with enough supplies to last three days."

"Should I pack swimwear?"

"Naturally. Excellent suggestion darling."

12:07 Friday afternoon Henry fired up the gas grill, then adjourned to return moments later carrying a massive white Styrofoam container. From it withdrawing lunch ingredients placing them on heater's grate.

"Closing upper lid and decreasing temperature. Everything should heat through perfectly now. Grab us a couple cold beers and follow me. Got something gargantuan inside for your eyes only."

"Oh, really? Guess my wife was right."

Hoisting garage door,

"Feast eyes on that beauty. She is my most valuable possession."

"Whew! A car."

Glaring back over his left shoulder with complete disgust,

"No one calls 1958 Corvettes, scandalous names. Totally restored her afterwards with original equipment."

"After what?"

"Ginny's collision. Losing one of my sleek women was bad enough."

"Ginny must have been your fiancé?"

"Mmm. Gorgeous, sexy. Downright impulsive. Ran through a flashing red light. Never stopped."

"So sorry."

"Expired. Died that day myself. Inside."

"Stunning black exterior. Silver cove. Elegant pebble-grain red interior. Probably very powerful."

"283 cubic inch engine. Dual quads. 4 speed, correct shifter."

"Reincarnation."

"Only wish I could somehow bring Ginny back in like fashion."

Henry sighed. Shook his head.

"We had best leave."

Barbecued chicken drumsticks tasted divine. Punched clock 1:09. Scrutinized informative catalogue.

# Tough decision

3:07 Saturday afternoon checked into Williams Inn. Traditional King-size room. Free parking. Nice clean place. Dined. (Luxurious restaurant.) Lounged in hot tub. Swam. (Indoor pool.) Not cheap, but reasonable. Ski area close-by held no interest. Checked out Monday morning at 10:45. Drove south on route #7. Arrived home fully recharged. Unpacked.

Punched clock 8:30 Tuesday January 22. Withdrew $167 at main office 34 minutes later. Ambled downhill.

"Good morning Jim. Brought one third total price down payment as promised."

"Thanks Pukka. Care for coffee?"

"Will pass my friend. Already enjoyed two cups."

"Alright then. Starting immediately on your recent modifications."

Returned to my office. Performed several assessments. Immediate commander was standing in doorway.

"Hello. Busy hey?"

"Never too busy for higher supervisors. Come take a look at some startling calculations."

"Ok. Do anything special over this past long weekend?"

"Spent two days in a local hotel. Carol enjoyed herself immensely. We had loads of fun relaxing."

"Lucky man. Very. What is Henry looking at?"

Explaining consumed 15 minutes or more.

"Where would anyone mount all these smaller units?"

"Location matters little. Many available areas exist. That is what I am investigating presently."

"$42,000 present setup versus $17,500 proposed."

"Absolutely correct. $24,500 savings per every unit sold."

"According to these startling algorithms, efficiency would increase by 200% minimum."

"Identical deductions. Same exact conclusion."

"This is big. Really big."

"Stole Ed Sullivan's line, Huh?"

1:06 Thursday phone rang. (Mr. Whittick seeking further instructions.)

"Pacify yourself. Will be there immediately."

Hit up main office. Extricated $330. Hurried downhill. Allocated funds.

"Much appreciated."

"My pleasure. Let's determine restrictive head loss through rectangular orifice."

Performed several adjustments. Recorded all pertinent results on notepad. Facts proved the new design was a complete success."

"Will you be having more projects soon?"

"Definitely. Might want to consider hiring four or five more talented employees."

"Awesome! When does this venture take place?"

"Ordering 56 sand separators that arrive within 40 days. Installing them should provide ample labor."

"You are a miracle worker."

"Only doing my job."

3:26 returned to main office. Tried withdrawing $73,500. Sharon hesitated.

"Please wait. Must get your request approved."

"Who are you contacting?"

"Company vice president."

Twenty five grueling minutes transpired. Returned to office smiling. Placed toll-free long distance phone call. Prattled with Ms. Denise Meadows in sales department for nearly half an hour."

"Yes. No price changes. $1,250 apiece. Includes shipping. 5% sales tax. How many?"

"Did I stutter? 56. Should receive your bank check early next week."

"Thanks Mr. Carpenter. Will there be anything else?"

"Not today."

"We appreciate your business. Bye for now."

Wednesday February 23, 1994 10:37 a.m. immediate supervisor appeared distressed entering my office.

"Good morning Henry."

"Grandpa died last night."

"Oh! Sorry to hear that."

"Many reforms take place. Everything transfigures."

"Am I laid off?"

"Humph. On the contrary you inherit my subsistent position with Sparkling Waters."

"Abandoning this blue-chip corporation?"

"Not leaving. Moving up in company ranks. Vice president. Only Karmen contrasts higher up on totem pole. Well? Accepting paramount investiture?"

"Indoctrinating offer. Whew! Very tempting indeed, but I prefer designer/draftsman responsibilities."

"Crazy? Salaried $80,000 per year conjuncture is yours. Merely accept."

"Hmm. Must consider things and evaluate my current position. Tendering any premeditated deadline?"

"Friday noon. Allocates two full days. Discuss comprehensive proposal with Carol."

**Phone rings.**

"Choose wisely. We could use those extraordinary talents."

**Ring.**

"Probably right."

"Heading out. Bye."

**Ring.**

"Hello."

"Jim Wittick here. 18-wheeler delivered 56 sand separators this early morning. Thought you might be investigative."

"Perfect. See you soon."

**Scene ends. Reopens 11:14 as Mr. Whittick analyzes blueprint silently.**

"How much money will everything cost?"

"112 holes at $25 each. That comes to $2,800. Plus parts, installation, labor. Hmm. $5,300 altogether."

"Done deal. Start unpacking 14 boxes. Will have your down payment about 2:00 o'clock."

**Arrived home 5:35. Checked mailbox. Proceeded up driveway. Parked. Climbed stairway. Heard wife's Golf approaching.**

"Hi Honey. Decline customary overtime tonight?"

"Yes dear. Feel trapped. Must somehow make a complex decision within 40 hours. Will discuss related details and various options after supper."

**Friday March 1 immediate supervisor knocked on office door at 11:29.**

"Please enter. Good morning Henry."

"Surely you have decided to accept my proposal. Welcome aboard."

"Much work remains incorporating these upscale modifications. Am a very good designer/draftsman. Enjoyed my role within the research and development area although brief. I am sorry. Declining your generous offer."

# Feeling lucky.

Monday September 11, 1995 10:06 a.m. company vice president knocked on my office door, then entered.

"Good morning Henry."

"Have done well Pukka. What project are you working on presently?"

"Wrapping things up. Should complete revising Installation & Maintenance manual within 12 hours."

"Sparkling Waters successfully acquired our new patent. Dismantling the research and development group. Came to tell senior designer personally."

"Appreciate that my friend. Start packing now?"

"Was hoping otherwise. Must incorporate design modifications somehow. Mind staying on another year?"

"Same pay?"

"Whew! Drive a hard bargain there buddy. Hmm. $25 per hour. Alright, but no overtime."

"Done deal."

Punched out 5:01. Stopped at Williamstown supermarket. purchased whole broiled chicken, potato wedges, dozen red roses. Drove home. Checked empty mailbox. Parked beside Volkswagen. Gathered both bags. Went upstairs.

"My thoughtful hubby supplied supper. Great!"

"Bought this small rotisserie chicken and some gorgeous plants."

"They are beautiful. Thanks Honey. Any special occasion? Oh no! Got laid off?"

"Henry vaporized research and development altogether. They possess their new patent now. My position has drastically changed. No more overtime."

"Be thankful work remains available. Set out plates while your wife locates flower vase."

Tuesday afternoon 1:45 finished plotting out 57-page instruction book. Someone knocked.

"Please enter."

"Pukka Carpenter. Meet your new commander, Peter Franz."

We shook hands.

"Coordinating efforts, Pukka will be moving into our central drafting area tomorrow."

"Where might that be located?"

"Lower mansion's second floor."

"Any special time?"

"New hours are eight to five. Stop by early. Before 11:00 o'clock. Well, must leave now."

"Bye Mr. Franz."

"Too formal my friend. Call me Peter. Bye."

"He is a brilliant man. You should get along well together. Brought small tokens of appreciation."

"Two Sparkling Waters porcelain cups. Both red."

"Look closer, locating your name."

"Pukka Carpenter. Senior Design Specialist."

"Take your small refrigerator also."

"Thanks Henry."

"Be sure to back up all your files before leaving."

"Already have. Five CD's altogether."

Wednesday 8:25 a.m. light rain posed little problem. Cleaned out my office. Loaded personal possessions into pickup truck. Drove downhill. Climbed flight of stairs. Placed time card on right-hand side of clock. Had two directions available. Walked left.

"Good morning. Is this the main drafting section? Looking for Peter Franz."

"His cubicle resides over there. Your name please."

Handed her my Sparkling Waters cup.

"Punctual hey? Pamela Manikowski here, group secretary. Let me unveil new work station."

"Will I lose my telephone extension?"

"No. Should be up and running later this afternoon."

New boss stood at my cubicle's entrance.

"Hi Peter. Loaded all new files into this computer. Awaiting first assignment."

"Brought four sketches. Look them over, then design a subsequent catwalk."

"One eighth inch thick diamond plate should suffice for flooring."

"Expensive though. Use regular mild steel."

"Might get slippery or even rust."

"Employ sand-stipple paint. Avoid full-length threaded bolts."

"Always do. They cost double with minimized shear stress."

"This exemplifies rush project. Only have 32 working hours."

"No problem. Oh! Here is revised Installation-Maintenance manual. Check it over, then make 10 books for our vice president."

Telephone repairman required 15 minutes. Pukka investigated plotter, large copy machine. Saw coffee club's setup. 20 cents per cup. Two choices: Regular Maxwell house or Sanka naturally decaffeinated. Elected 50-50 blend. Tossed quarter aboard collection basket. Noticed repairman leaving. Returned to cubicle. Phone rang.

"Hello."

"Hi. Pam speaking. Just verifying your extension works. Should be all set for incoming calls now."

"Thanks Pam. Will there be anything else?"

"Actually yes. Must submit vacation request. Entitled to 15 days. Use them or they are lost."

"Plan investigating my calendar. Next Monday soon enough for accurate response?"

"Perfect. We prefer solid blocks over individual days."

"So noted. Bye."

Punched time clock 5:03. Drove home. Noticed wife's car. Stopped at mailbox, then continued up driveway.

"Hi darling. Been here long?"

"Maybe 10 minutes. Hope your day was less hectic than mine. No mail tonight?"

"Nothing. Sounds like you are ready for another extended vacation and before long."

"Serious?"

"Yes dear. We leave Friday October 10. Return November 2."

"Any special destination?"

"Your option. Could take a cruise to Freeport on Grand Bahama Island or head north observing spectacular fall foliage."

"Feeling lucky. They have legalized gambling in the Bahamas?"

"Sure. Many casinos. Could get more conch chowder. Hit a few Hotels. Do some dancing. Maybe play golf."

"How much money would that excursion cost?"

"$4,800 plus gambling expenses."

"Wow! We can not afford spending excessive amounts of cash right now. Must purchase four ton of rice coal plus 1,000 gallons of propane soon. Let's vacation home. We could take a few local gambling junkets. Foxwoods, Mohegan Sun."

"Yes. My wife is right. Want me to start cooking supper?"

"Anything special?"

"Reuben sandwiches, spicy chili. Must use up our leftovers."

"Sounds great! Hmm. Submitting those days off tomorrow. Anything exciting take place at work?"

"Moved into lower mansion. Must design a catwalk within limited schedule. If stopping by visiting, climb their stairway. Second floor. Then turn left."

"We have no thousand island dressing. Only chunky blue cheese."

"Plan on improvising anyhow. Grab some frozen chili, then heat it in our microwave oven."

# Mohegan Sun casino.

Saturday October 14 caught King Ward bus headed for Connecticut. Shelled out $50 for our combined round-trip fares. Excellent deal. Each passenger received bonus packages at Mohegan Sun: $10 coupon toward food or retail, plus $15 in free bets. Arrived 10:28 a.m. Redeemed our vouchers immediately. Played $2-$4 Texas Holdem poker table until noon. Stopped for lunch. Nothing fancy. Hamburg specials, french fries, ginger ale. Tasty food. Left $10 tip. Located two adjoining vacant seats at $4-$8 table. Ahead serious amount of money and peeking Ace, four of spades, dealer flopped 5,6,7 also spades. Someone raised $30. All others called. Pukka wagered all-in. Lost everything. Opponent held straight flush. Luckily, monstrous hand winner was Carol.

"Good job. Now cash out. Nearly 4:00. Must go."

Sunday morning Preacher Joe performed church ceremonies. Was informed Reverend Stone had relocated to Florida and new hours would go into effect. Instead of 9:00 until 10:00, future customary services begin at 2:00.

Monday: Harvested apples and pears. Stored 23 bushel altogether. Tuesday: I drove wife's car north on Route #7 without any particular destination. Spotted intriguing tourist area on left side of road. Stopped.

"Where are we?"

"Not positive. Maybe East Dorset?"

"Pond's water appears rich green. Looks very scenic. Let's hike around it. Bring our camera."

"Sure."

Wednesday: Sold 18 bushel of fruit to Norman's Variety. Mostly pears. Apples also. Collected $112.50. Thursday: Coal pellet stove malfunctioned. Purchased new electric motor. Ouch! Dispensed $92.40. Friday: My sister, Marlene, called. Jack sold their Ocala Arabian horse ranch They are relocating to another enormous 20- acre spread in Stamford, Vermont. Saturday: Bus arrived exactly 10:30. Soon we were both seated beside each other at a $10-$20 Texas Holdem table with $720 worth of chips apiece. Perhaps, the man wearing green sweater was bluffing again. Will never know.

"$350."

"Fold."

"Tossing mine."

"Grab all your remaining chips. Lunchtime."

Wife nodded toward dealer. Approaching restaurant,

"What are you ordering?"

"Sirloin steak, french fries, salad. Maybe decaffeinated coffee."

"Sounds good. Same here. Doing an awesome number Pukka. Must have over $2,000. Impressive. Already lost about $500 myself. That guy is surely bluffing. Every hand. Humph. Crazy wagers. Jerk. Think we should move?"

"Might become necessary darling. Getting crowded. Probably will have trouble locating adjoining seats."

Meal was excellent. Deposited $20 tip. Surprisingly, only four players remained on our original table. Mr. Green Sweater possessed tons of chips. Only waited through two episodes. Large blind struck. Slid appropriate  token forward. Hmm. Ace, King off suit. Both red. Ace of diamonds.

"Call."

"Fold."

"Out."

"$650."

"Call."

"Color this one gone."

Ace clubs, 7 diamonds, King spades.

"$750."

"Raise $1,000."

"Fold. Well, that was entertaining. Profitable day. Hmm. Am off . Quitting. Slot machines keep beckoning."

"Excellent maneuver Honey. Your wife has lost enough. Should quit immediately. Our transportation will be arriving soon. Can ill afford missing the bus. Already 2:35. "

"Still have much time. Nearly two hours remaining. Need some tokens?"

"Way ahead. Please listen to me. Quit before relinquishing all."

"Humph! Tomorrow is another day. Cashing out."

Sunday morning heavy rain pummeled Williamstown. Carol fried sausage plus eggs over easy for breakfast. Later we made short journey to church. Deposited twin $20 bills aboard collection plate.

Arrived in Stamford, Vermont punching 4:45 well prepared to formulate supper for Jack and Marlene. Very impressed with their massive house.

"Welcome gang. Please enter. Pardon these cardboard boxes. Still unpacking."

"Hello sis. Not raining here. Surprising. Where might your kitchen be located? This cartage weighs bunches."

"Follow me. Buy everything within your customary supermarket?"

"Supplied plenty, but left two or three items. Run along now, allowing workable space."

"Hubby should return before darkness strikes. He presently mows lower pasture."

"Still have all those black Arabian horses?"

"Naturally. Only sold three. Transported all others. Kept my champion. Come take a look out patio windows."

Ladies adjourned leaving volunteer chef ample space for investigating efficient cooking area. By 7:00 major labor stood accomplished. Parlor door opens,

"Hi Pukka. Women there with you?"

"They evacuated. Should return soon though. Supper is nearly ready."

"Watched you driving our new tractor home. Were advancing very slowly. Experience any problems?"

"Simply takes time learning how reddish-orange powerful beast operates. Cuts super. Will complete mowing tomorrow. Could have finished manicuring lower field tonight, but was getting hungry."

"Need assistance Honey? Mashing potatoes or anything?"

"Very thoughtful darling. Locate plates, silverware, napkins. Then adorn dining room's table, but please hurry. Steaks begin broiling immediately. Hope everyone likes theirs medium-rare."

"Prefer mine mooing still."

"Poses little inconvenience. Will wait two minutes before starting your rib-eye beauty."

"Investigate refrigerator contents. Should be four cans of Natural Ice beer left. Help yourself."

"Unnecessary. Keep them. Brought cold 6-pack of Rolling Rock brews. Unopened Liebfraumilch bottle also."

"Never even heard that term before. Hmm. Some type of wine?"

"Exactly correct. Not having any personally. Brought semi-sweet white version especially for you."

"Will try some if your wife does. California grown?"

"No Mar. Imported from Germany. Slightly expensive. Want some now?"

"What say? Shall we?"

"Why not? Hubby drives both of us home later. Right Honey?"

"Absolutely. Must employ a corkscrew. Have one available sis?"

"Hmm. Well maybe. Yes. Be right back."

"Experience any trouble locating this place?"

"Child's play actually. Received explicit directions. Might best de-cork blue bottle for both ladies. Rather busy currently myself. Must coordinate cooking efforts."

**Scene ends. Reopens Monday 8:30 a.m.**

"Good morning baby brother. Where is your soul mate?"

"Showering. Already took mine. Brewed large pot of Green Mountain coffee. Care for some?"

"Perhaps. Only half cup though. Horses require tending. Frying onions?"

"Chopped two small ones. Added them to simmering home fries."

"Glad you accepted our overnight invitation. You are both welcome to drop by anytime."

# Winter provisions.

Tuesday morning October 16. Usurped costly deliveries: 4-ton of bulk rice coal. Took until 5:45 relocating huge mound, then close basement's door. Local gas company filled 1,000 gallon white propane tank.

Wednesday: Using $5 off coupon, purchased 14-pound frozen turkey. Also bought massive butternut squash, eight jumbo Idaho baking potatoes, plus six-pound turnip. Stopped over my parent's house at 3:15. Momma met us promptly addressing parlor's entrance door.

"Hi Al. Supplying assorted Thanksgiving donations."

"Awesome! Undoubtedly hefty parcels. Hurry. Set those bags aboard kitchen table."

"Hey? Great! Almost called last night. Got an outstanding business proposal."

"Really Dad? What type?"

"Black Angus beef. We could split total price equally. Can purchase an entire hind quarter for only $1.39 per pound hanging weight. All professionally cut, wrapped, and labeled."

"Been spending enormous amounts of money recently Pukka. Still have enough reserved to pay your monthly mortgage?"

"Sure thing. Carol? Bring our checkbook?"

"Unnecessary maneuver. Use one of three blank checks stashed aboard Hubby's wallet."

"Ok. Will temporarily require operating blue or black inked pen."

"Possess many over there on that shelf. Help yourself."

"Spotted them. This should not take long."

Moments slipped away.

"Returning shortly with paid-in-full receipts November's also."

"What are you doing now?"

"Spending additional funds. Here Dad. Our half should comprise roughly $250. Will work out pertinent details later. Buy the hind quarter."

"Done deal. Be sure to stop by Saturday afternoon. Anyone care for soda? Root beer or ginger ale?"

"None for me."

"Same response here. Leaving soon anyway."

"Back again with promised receipts. Who gets these?"

"I will commandeer them. Thanks."

"Possess adequate storage space within Grandma's old freezer?"

"Do not trust ancient machines. Insane gamble. Could readily lose entire contents. Bought another new version with many sliding trays. An enormous 21 cubic foot chest type. Hubby dickered price and successfully harvested his whopping $125 instant cash rebate. Colossal package deal. Free delivery, plus removal of antiquated model."

"Peace of mind always comes with its stiff price tag."

"Apparently true Honey. Shelled out nearly $1,200 altogether addressing frozen food compartment. Humph. We have not even splurged filling it yet."

"Just secured numerous corn-fed beef steaks and roasts. Probably will not overburden your new 21 cubic foot freezer, but project has officially launched. I know another farm where pigs are raised. Might stop tomorrow checking their basic prices. Should know more by Friday."

"Sounds good Harold. Will keep in touch. See you Saturday afternoon if not sooner. Heading home now. Bye Althea."

"Bye Carol. Enjoy this lovely day's remaining hours. Take care son. Drive carefully."

Thursday afternoon we rented a 505 sailboat and toured across Pontoosac Lake. Friday 6:20 p.m. phone rang.

"Hello?"

"Good evening young lady. There has been a change of plans. Minor dilemma. Harold picked up the packaged meat a short while ago. Can our neighbors drop by tonight?"

"Definitely. Hmm. Pukka showers presently. See you about 7:00?"

"Perfect. Bye."

"Pukka? Hurry along. We must leave soon."

Backed pickup truck to within two yards of double-wide door. Lowered tailgate. Accomplished our garage positions through side entrance.

"Nice seeing next-house neighbors. Welcome to well adorned dispatch shop."

"Hi Althea. Have anything discounted today?"

"Certainly. Romping blue light special. Prime, aged Black Angus beef. Only $210 for twin hefty boxes."

"How heavy?"

"Unsure. Over 70 pounds apiece. Carted them all without assistance."

"Are all four cardboard containers equally divided?"

"Yes. Disproportionate initially, Al helped for over half an hour repacking them. Who gets this $40 refund?"

"My husband."

"Oh! Money? Thanks Dad. Went sailing yesterday. You would not believe the ridiculous proportions of a 505 sailboat's spinnaker. Impressive. Simply awesome."

"Sounds like my son and daughter-in-law have been enjoying their vacation."

"Immensely. Was on a supportive trapeze at least three times. Could view boat's entire bottom. Only tips of my topsider sneakers remained aboard."

"Harold has lifted enough for one day. Hear me Pukka? On your own, son. Commence lugging."

"Raising main entrance with the press of a button. There. Much shorter jaunt young man."

Successfully carted both installments, then hoisted tailgate.

"Stay here Carol. Returning soon. Probably within 35 minutes."

"Want help?"

"Unnecessary. Enjoy visiting."

Scene ends. Reopens 8:00 o'clock in parent's kitchen.

"Eat supper yet? Could broil some hamburgers."

"Another time Al. Hubby fried pickled tripe, reheated spaghetti sauce, then boiled linguine merely three hours ago. My first introduction to sour tripe. Tasted alright, but chewy."

"Harold? Update our guests concerning yesterday's findings."

"Findings hey? Hmm. Probably discovered gold on your property. Or struck oil perhaps."

"No such luck Carol. Longest boar these ancient eyes have ever seen. About a half ton. Owner, Jim Hathaway, estimates slightly more. Amazing proportions. Neutered male. Must purchase entire pork vault though."

"How much does this Mr. Hathaway ask price-wise?"

"Only $1.09 per pound hanging weight."

"What thinking Honey? Same deal as last? Still have abundant freezer space?"

"Have no practical use for any enormous pig's head. Do not enjoy pork liver's bitter flavor much either."

"Your sister's fussy Chihuahuas both love all types of liver. Norman's Variety store will undoubtedly purchase entire long-snout head from us for some reasonable price. Rita constantly wheels-deals with various customers. Might even swap for delicious hot dogs."

"Right as rain. They paid mullah for Carpenter pears and apples. Wallet searching for something Moneybags?"

"Decisive blank check. Remind me after to grab a few more. Make it out to Dad quickly, before I reconsider."

"Humph. Any clues? What amount?"

"$500 should efficiently protect our 50% of total price commitment."

# Baked stuffed pork chops.

Saturday October 21 11:50 a.m. Carol drove Route 7 south. Knew we had reached destination. Thronging parking lot. Soon, we located food concession. Ordered identical plates: Six grilled Bratwurst, sauerkraut, and hot mustard. Total price: $14. Sat at wooden table directly adjoining dance area. Waitress dressed in black skirt held up by 4-inch wide black suspenders, white shirt approached our location.

"May I get you anything to drink?"

"Certainly. Hmm. Pitcher of Bodenwohrer, two glasses."

Nodding acknowledgement, she turned-walked away. Five minutes later waitress returned.

"$7.50 please."

Shelled out $10 bill.

"Close enough. Keep any change."

Band took their positions aboard raised podium. Five musicians altogether: Oboe, Alto (tenor) horn, guitar, male vocalist, accordion.

"Enjoying your lunch?"

"Delicious. Wonder what ingredients are involved making these wieners."

"Veal sausage, nutmeg, lemon zest."

Accordion player introduced group members. Experienced difficultly understanding foreign accent. They tuned their various instruments. Not sure. Primary rendition's  title sounded like Volkszinger. Was a waltz. Very strong words escaped us both, but melody sounded patriotic. Would have danced if others did. That was not the case. Everyone enthusiastically applauded. Band performed three more tunes. Still no dance area takers.

"Let's shake booty."

"Ok. Next tune."

Oktoberfest song rang out. Danced while vigorous polka blared. Many others joined frivolity. Arrived at my parent's house 5:30. Entered garage through side door.

"Good evening Ma."

"Howdy son. Harold left with your truck nearly four hours ago. Expect his return anytime now. Wait. Is that not him backing up? Yes. Am convinced. Push ivory button, raising main entrance. Perfect. Much facilitated. Traveling alone tonight?"

"Hardly. Wife rests awhile out in our car."

"Been drinking?"

"Sparingly. Only had four glasses of beer myself. Wife readily doubled my skimpy consumption. We have new clientele approaching. "

"Welcome Carol. Hmm. Feeling somewhat tipsy hey?"

"Hi Al. Was a fantastic day. Returning shortly. Must tinkle."

"Going also. Please follow me."

Women exit. Scene ends. Reopens later that evening at 8:35.

"Homecoming complete. Have adequate freezer space?"

"Yes Althea, but not much remains. Whew! Six teeming boxes. Did some bartering with Rita. Got 20 pounds of delicious hot dogs from Norman's store. Brought your half. Set those down someplace Pukka. We owe anything?"

"No idea."

"Thanks for reminding me Carol. Delight taking possession of your generous $23 rebate."

"Sure about that?"

"Absolutely. Was charged $954 altogether. 876 pounds hanging weight. Only cost $1.09 per pound. Very good price. Truly an exceptional deal."

"Here Honey. Replenish your wallet. After all, you splurged for both pitchers of German brew."

"Plan donating this stash aboard church's collection plate tomorrow."

"Know something? I have never seen pork chops sliced so thick before. Totally awesome!"

"Thinner versions end up dried out. Butcher asked our preference. Told him 2½ inch thick slices."

"Makes perfect sense Harold."

"My mom served the ultimate best cuisine. Pukka inherited her priceless cookbook. Amazing cuisine. Try some. You will not be even slightly disappointed. Fantastic recipe."

Grandma's stuffed pork chops:

4 thick chops sliced from fat end to bone.

1 cup: finely chopped onion, celery heart.

2 cups: dry bread crumbs, apple sauce, chicken broth.

½ pound (Two sticks.) unsalted butter.

1 teaspoon: dried thyme, ground black pepper, paprika, Bell's seasoning

1½ tablespoon minced parsley.

Large skillet: First stick of melted butter, onion, celery. Sauté. When tender, remove from heat. Stir in apple sauce, half of chicken broth, bread crumbs, thyme, pepper, paprika, Bell's seasoning, parsley. Blend very well. Generously spoon mix into each pocket. Secure closure employing lengthy wooden toothpicks. Melt remaining butter in recycled skillet. Brown both sides of meat. Place aboard greased baking pan. Pour all remaining broth over chops. Cover. Bake (350 degrees.) 40 minutes. Check for doneness. Remove toothpicks. Serve with fresh salad and baked potato.

# One step away.

Monday October 28, 2003 9:05 a.m. Parlor phone signals: 'Incoming Message'. Wife attentively answers on second ring. Hurriedly blurts,

"Pukka? Hurry! Who sings country hit: Tough Little Boys?  Barry, Jerry, Larry somebody?"

"Wrong. Gary. Close dear. Gary Allan performs that gem. Great tune. Strong lyrics. Sad though."

One moment later, soul mate rejoins kitchen's work force.

"Emptied overburdened dishwasher hey?"

"Sure thing. Sparkling clean and Martini-dry glasses. Who inquired concerning specific male vocalists?"

"Beverly presently attempts capturing some allusive radio station prize."

"Sounds like foolishness. Wasted effort. Advertisement gimmicks. Probably fixed."

"Doubt that. Realize something Honey? Six tergiversation days left. Arrange extended vacation plans yet?"

"Hmm. Think we should take my brother-in-law up on his generous offer? Head south, camping awhile?"

"Three weeks late, Know-it-all. Your sister's equine strutting bid already forfeited."

"Equus ferus caballus."

"Latin? Paltry linguistic matter. Distinguished worthily-conditioned animal belly-flopped high-stakes début."

"But astonishing horse normally flourishes. Five Regional uncontested championships. Triumphed first place every occasion. 100% successful until just recently. Humph. At least he made an impressive splash."

"Would have attended those local Arabian horse shows personally, if granted adequate time from employment responsibilities. Louisville, Kentucky reposes far away. Marlene's black stallion lost the National Meet there. Only mustered Freedom Hall's fourth position."

"Ouch! No one ever tells me anything. Three weeks ago? Major disappointment. Marlene must feel crushed."

Phone rings, then again.

"Carpenter's mortuary. You stab them. We slab them."

Awaited further communication as many seconds slipped oblivion-bound. Old Cowboy finally abandoned yet another sinking ship.

"Returning momentarily. Receptive mailbox beckons."

Carol nods accreditation while waving right-handed, further exemplifying comprehensive acknowledgement.

"Any interesting mail?"

"Absolutely nothing. Might be too early. Will check again later. Who initiated last electronic conversation?"

"Lucky Beverly, country music station's number seven responder. Nailed performer's correct handle. Amazing. Spoke very excitedly. Difficult making logical sense. Thanked us both repeatedly. Want beef or pork thawed out for supper?"

"Neither darling. Why consume our winter storage prematurely? Much inclement weather remains ahead. You dislike fresh caught rainbow trout?"

"Most anglers surrendered to other pass times already. Excessively early for ice fishing. Who are you calling?"

Scene ends. Reopens at 5:49 p.m. as John Linpav responding to his door bell opens main entrance.

"Hi Jack. We made it here slightly behind schedule. Hope you have not eaten supper yet."

"Welcome gang. Set those bags down aboard kitchen's shelf. Been expecting your attendance."

"Good evening. Heard the bad report about finishing poorly in Kentucky."

"Almost made some real profits. Horse ran out of gas. Only took two backward steps. Another, and he would have dominated."

"Hubby taught me how to cast a fly rod. Was dead calm this afternoon. Seemed as though Onota Lake's surface boiled. We caught  15 lovely trout altogether. Only kept enough for this evening's meal. One jumbo salmon nearly 27 inches in length. Already filleted and oven ready."

"Don't care much for fish personally. Always preferred red meats. Especially beef steaks cooked exceedingly rare."

"Diet include baked pork? We also supplied four enormous hocks singed and par-boiled."

"Never tried those before. They tough chewing?"

"Hmm. Somewhat, but I already tenderized the lot. Will braise them now to perfection."

"Best get started Honey. Getting late. Everyone is positively famished. Where might your better half be Jack?"

"Probably still on our patio. Been sewing some type of quilt out there. Let's go investigate, while Master chef performs."

Grandma's pork hocks:

4 fresh pork hocks (Singed over an open flame, removing possible hairs.)

3½ quarts water

6 celery stalks, potatoes, medium onions, carrots, rutabagas (Bite-sized chunks.)

Bay leaf or leaves as desired.

Racing boil: ½ hour uncovered. Skim off surface, then slow boil another 45 minutes employing ajar cover. Drain, saving all veggies and broth: Provides a flavorful stew.

Burnish:

3 tablespoons corn oil, clover honey

1½ teaspoons garlic powder

Bake: 35 minutes (350 degrees.) Glaze often.

"Thanks for calling this morning. Big sister was feeling melancholic."

"Good evening Mar. Perfect timing. Set out plates and customary utensils. Only have 11 minutes."

"Beverly was fortunate earlier today. Won an electronic AM-FM clock radio manufactured by Sound Design."

"Guess that maneuver comprehensively disproves bogus theories."

"Which of you caught the enormous salmon?"

"Carol, but yours truly netted him."

"Humph. Classic example of student surpassing teacher."

"Still have much to learn accomplishing that feat. My private counselor released 12 rainbow trout, while novice only tossed back three. Heard you are an ordained minister these days."

"True enough. Simply proves, God works in mysterious ways."

"He stopped my champion's backward motion. Nearly triumphed. Performed well, but lost. One step away."

Sometimes unexpected things happen. Door bell rings.

"Need assistance Honey?"

"Negative dear. Got everything under control."

"When finished with your present glazing effort, turn around. Company arrived. Your parents have located us."

"Really? What a delightful coincidence. Please hurry. Furnish two more place settings."

"No coincidence Cowboy. I invited Mom and Dad for supper."

"Did Hubby provide adequate foodstuff?"

"Plenty. Only frying one fillet tonight. Conveyed much stew. Two full quarts. Baking seven Idaho potatoes."

"Seven? Why so many? Oh! Never mind. Home fries addressing breakfast hey?"

"Exactly correct Carol. Already predetermined serving those golden cavaliers, the lingering fillet, four 8-ounce Delmonico steaks, plus cheddar cheese omelets."

"Want me running back, hauling our small brown suitcase indoors? Only brought one."

"Unnecessary toil. Will grab it myself after everything tranquilizes. Bestowing completeness immediately. Go inform everyone, then be seated."

Twenty minutes elapse.

"Needs salt. Very tender and flavorful. Severely overcooked though. Thanks anyway Pukka. Perhaps, Harold would care for another."

"Ready Dad? Only one left."

"Had enough. Excellent feast. Must save room anticipating dessert. Love your mom's pineapple upside-down cake."

# Doubtful speculation.

Tuesday 9:45 a.m. During breakfast Marlene starts chuckling for no apparent reason. Offers enlightenment.

"Found Dad's frustration hilarious. Neither divulged what Carol employed to deceive her trophy salmon."

"Instructor Pukka selected our prosperous dry flies. Apprentice merely attached the diminutive attraction."

"Well, must leave immediately. Lengthy drive ahead. Another house closing. Becket, Massachusetts this time. Stopping twice on return expedition. Purchasing sugar cubes. Oats also. Positive 80 pounds will suffice?"

"Absolutely 100% sure. Each Arabian only receives a pint of vitality every morning. Good luck with sales."

Jack nods acknowledgement. Hastens departure.

"Must tend my enchanting horses now."

"Already packed brown suitcase. We should get underway soon."

"Rinsed off soiled plates and utensils. Slip them aboard your dishwasher later. Bye sis. Heading back directly."

"Thanks baby brother. Excelled cooking both fabulous meals. Superb omelet. Delicious fish. Everything you attributed savored wonderful. Truly divine talent. Call ahead first making sure we are going to be here. Drop in again anytime. Drive safely."

Scene ends. Reopens Wednesday 4:30 p.m.

"You said a few minutes. Been nearly 40. Norman's variety store resides close-by. Do not understand."

"Occupied darling. Rita was swamped with customers. She finally refunded all the wooded baskets. Just lugged them down into our basement. Been tending Grandma's recipe?"

"Four times per hour. Only added water twice. Smells delicious. Hope your parents appreciate them. We have nothing drinkable to bring. Buy any beer?"

"Oh! Forgot. Will run back there again."

"Hmm. With me as passenger this trip. Let's go."

Grandma's special beans:

3 cups dried navy beans

Water (As required for soaking plus 2¾ cups.)

Heaping tablespoon baking soda

Hefty dash of liquid smoke

2 pounds sliced bacon (Quartered into reasonable lengths.)

12 ounces salt pork (½ inch cubes.)

3 large onions (Finely chopped.)

1 red Bell pepper (Coarsely chopped.)

1 teaspoon mustard

1½ tablespoons molasses or brown sugar

6 cloves

4 ounces cider vinegar

8 ounces tomato juice

3 Granny Smith apples (½ inch cubes.)

2 tablespoons vegetable oil

Inspect, thoroughly wash beans. Soak 10 hours employing adequate portion of water, baking soda.

16-quart kettle (Or larger.)

Boil bacon and salt pork 15 minutes. Drain. Add oil, onion, Bell pepper. Sauté until peppers become tender. Add beans, liquid smoke, mustard, molasses, vinegar, tomato juice, water, apples, cloves. Blend well employing long-handled wooden spoon. Cover. Bake at 350 degrees 75 minutes. Stir occasionally. Uncover. Continue cooking 1¾ hours. Check periodically, dispensing additional water as needed.

Entered through garage's side entrance together punching 5:30.

"Hi Althea. Sorry about arriving late."

"Harold remains frustrated still. Foolish reaction. What is the big secret anyway? Anglers should stick together, sharing their fortunate experiences."

"Absolutely correct Ma. Total foolishness on my part. Childish prank backfired."

"Hi neighbors. Was beginning to think maybe you were not showing up. Hand that kettle over son. Must start broiling hamburgers immediately anyhow."

"Marlene's quilting project looks beautiful. Will be worth serious money when her mission stands complete."

"Not positive, but can only presume one of her daughters will inherit that quilt. Be seated. Threw another salad together. Fabricated three lemon meringue pies for dessert. Used very scanty amount of powdered sugar. Maybe even your husband will try a thin sliver."

"Hmm. Doubtful speculation Althea. Unlikely ambition."

Thursday 3:25 p.m. Totally exhausted from climbing up and down extension ladders since sunup, Carol offers her official resignation.

"Honey? We collected several full baskets. Should probably leave remaining pears. Expectant deer enjoy them immensely. What is today's final tally?"

"28 bushel. Run upstairs now. Get some rest."

"Plan staying out here very long?"

"Another hour. Maybe two. Will join you around 6:00. Thaw something anticipating supper."

"Baked beans and boiled hot dogs sound edible?"

"Good choice. Chop an onion. Toast some rolls. Freeze the leftover beans in small portions afterwards. Can ill afford wasting food."

Transported six baskets into our basement. Sold all others. Excellent financial deal. Surprising.

"Welcome home. Things progress well?"

"Much better than anticipated. Here. Grab your 50%."

"60, 70, $85. Fantastic! Norman must have increased his fruit prices. You never cease to amaze me."

"Bartering with Rita? Mediocre occurrence. Been interchanging with both Norman and her many decades."

"Not that, Cowboy. Hubby devoured lemon meringue pie. Extremely unusual. Should have taken pictures."

"Was not at all sweet. Made Momma happy."

"Harold was radically elated also. Now he knows exactly which dry fly ascertained successful."

# Beef stew.

Monday May 17, 2004 Berkshire Eagle newspaper. Obituaries listed Harold G. Carpenter. Subsequent wake and funeral to be held Wednesday. My mom called at 6:55 p.m. She sounded despondent, mournful. Appeasing efforts on my part proved futile.

Friday after work Carol and I ventured next door.

"Good evening Althea."

"Hi. Brought two large cans of red sockeye salmon. Pink versions taste inferior."

"Great! Will compose a lovely salmon gravy addressing tomorrow's lunch. Form any supper plans yet? Making pork roast, potatoes, carrots, onions. Even have salad ingredients."

"Sounds excellent. Set out additional plates."

During our dining experience Momma bequeaths shocking news.

"Sold the house. Hope you find time to drop by, visiting this old lady fairly often."

"Which nursing home?"

"Humph. Wrong conclusion. Staying with Jack and Marlene in Stamford, Vermont."

"Relocating anytime soon?"

"13 days. Already finalized arrangements."

"Will you be alright financially?"

"Lost out on Harold's various pensions, but have my own. Worked nearly 43 years as postmaster. Also drove school bus. Accepted a hefty down payment on the antique Lincoln Continental. Pukka? Like your local job?"

"Immensely. Sure beats commuting 140 miles every day."

"Comparable pay?"

"Not really. Only get $14.50 per hour. Much overtime available though. Working five 10's plus Saturdays."

"Health insurance available?"

"Company deducts $318 every month for that privilege. Their 2-person family plan."

"Seems reasonable. Full dental included?"

"This particular engineering outfit offers no such item. Our teeth are in formidable shape. Cleanings only cost us $400 yearly."

"Cheap enough. Must feel humiliated son. Carol presently earns more money than her husband."

"Alarm clock buzzes attention at 5:45 a.m. Must head back before long. Help stockpile Althea's dishwasher."

"Pork roast was small. No idea visitors were showing up. Would have baked another lemon meringue pie."

"Last one contained little powdered sugar. Perfect. Construct another tomorrow. Expect our return approaching 7:00 or shortly thereafter. Intend supplying everything else. Bye."

Saturday 6:37 p.m. We parked beside an unfamiliar vehicle. Apparently, Momma was entertaining at least one other guest.

"Want me running back capturing additional steaks?"

"Premature still. Possibly later. Let's analyze our situation first. Grab plastic bag's donation off your back seat."

"Please enter."

"Bad pennies returned."

"Set those things aboard kitchen table."

"Anyone else here?"

"No. Donna went home 20 minutes ago."

"Who owns the nifty white Subaru station wagon?"

"Me. Needed dependable transportation."

"Pleasant looking package. Is your car brand new?"

"Yes. Awesome warrantee. Same unit Harold selected before he died."

"Excellent choice. Should deliver superior fuel efficiency."

"Sticker claims 26 mpg. 5-speed automatic transmission."

"Honey? Inaugurate cooking, while famished ladies investigate sensational acquisition."

Sunday morning we labored pruning our various fruit trees. Following directions offered, one quart of Citrus, Fruit & Nut Orchard Spray produced 13 gallons of finished product. This application controls wide ranges of fungal diseases and various insects. Attended church services afterwards. Returned home to construct beef stew, plus four Italian bread loaves.

Grandma's Beef Stew:

5 lbs. chuck roast (1½ inch chunks.)

¾ cup corn oil

4 peeled onions (1 inch cubes.)

2½ cups Red Mill flour or Bisquick gluten-free baking mix.

3 whole bay leaves, garlic cloves (Minced.)

64 ounces red table wine

80 ounces beef broth

¾ tablespoon rosemary

1¼ teaspoon thyme

1 lb. Carrots, parsnips, celery (Thick slices.)

8 potatoes (Quartered.)

Large kettle. Using corn oil, brown meat thoroughly, then remove temporarily. Sauté garlic-onion until tender stirring constantly. Dispense wine, beef broth, flour, rosemary, thyme. Simmer 8 minutes. Add carrots, parsnips, celery. Cover. Cook 20 minutes (Medium-high.) Toss beef and potatoes aboard. Continue cooking with cover another half hour. Decrease temperature slightly. (Medium-low.) Stir. Replace cover. Check back in 75 minutes.

Monday 6:35 p.m. Momma's embryonic transportation climbed our driveway. Both of us hastened down front stairway.

"Hey, look! Additional guests have arrived. Your brother, Robert. Donna also. Good thing you made bunches of stew yesterday afternoon. Running back upstairs. Setting out more bowls."

Scene ends. Reopens at 7:25. Everyone is seated around kitchen table.

"Wow! Déjà vous. Extraordinary familiar taste. Been awhile though. Exactly same as Grandma's version."

"Supplied plenty. Care for more Bobby?"

"Yes Carol. How could anyone refuse an invitation like that? Delicious."

"Anyone else?"

Everyone present accepts my wife's generous offer.

"Think Ma's new car will perform well next winter, when snow flies?"

"Should function superbly. Equipped with 17 inch tires and all-wheel drive."

# Side impact.

Sunday June 19, 2005 7:15 p.m. Phone rings. Wife answers. Talks with someone five minutes. Hangs up.

"Who was that?"

"Marlene. Your mother and Beverly are recovering there. Will explain fully momentarily. Remain composed."

"Recovering?"

"Yes. No one was seriously injured. Relax. Go open our last bottle of beer, then microwave TV dinners. Scrod, or Haddock."

"Ok. Will make something tasty. Enough for six hungry people. Head to Norman's Variety. Need celery, Dijon mustard, smoked bacon. Oh! Another 12-pack also. Coors Light or Michelob Ultra. Hurry. Store closes soon."

"Limited selection. Heading to Williamstown supermarket. Require anything else?"

"Nothing comes to mind. Drive safely."

Scene ends. Reopens 6:05 Monday evening. Inside Jack's Stamford ranch house, Momma tells her story.

"Vermont State Trooper waved us on. The pickup truck just kept coming. Your sister was driving. I thought my life was over. $5,000 worth of damage. Ambulance brought us to North Adams Regional Hospital for x-rays and observation."

"Glad you survived the crash. What were you doing in Pownal, Vermont?"

"Playing high-stakes bingo. Won $100. Hope that insane driver never sees another license."

"Was Beverly charged with anything?"

"Of course not. She was only advancing with caution, while following policeman's directions."

"Insurance will pay for damages. Get yourself a rental vehicle."

"Must evaluate things first. May quit driving altogether. Too many lunatics out there on our highways."

"Eat yet?"

"No Carol. Was not very hungry. Until now. Still feeling disoriented."

"Honey? Everyone is famished. Start cooking. Fabricate something mild without many spices."

"Here Pukka. $20. Go purchase groceries."

"Unnecessary Ma. Hold onto that money. Brought an ice chest chockfull of goodies. Returning shortly."

"Heard you sprayed your fruit trees. Will nasty poison contaminate apples and pears?"

"Special spray contains Bonide. Not sure, but think it will work admirably. Directions state: Discontinue use three days before harvesting fruit. Humph. Could probably drink the stuff."

"Would not advise executing that irrational practice. Could upset anyone's body chemistry. Permanently."

"Hey, look who joined our midst. Hi Jack. Momma was truly fortunate."

"Subaru Outback cars are amongst the safest vehicles on the road. Rated five stars. Purchasing that particular automobile saved their lives. Set your ice chest down. Bring more steaks?"

"Not tonight. Eight jumbo sesame rolls. Thick cheddar cheese slices. Over two pounds of fresh 90% extra-lean hamburger, Claussen Kosher dill spears, and much red-skin potato salad with bacon. Already chilled adequately."

Grandma's deluxe potato salad:

7 medium-sized red potatoes (Unpeeled. Scour, then cut into ¾ inch cubes.)

1 pound smoked bacon (Cut into inch lengths.)

1½ cups mayonnaise (More or less.)

6 hard-boiled eggs (De-shelled. Chopped.)

1 large onion, green bell pepper (Diced.)

3 celery stalks (Diced.)

8 ounces baby peas, pitted black olives

¾ tablespoon Dijon mustard

¼ teaspoon paprika, ground black pepper

Dash of garlic powder

Boil potatoes until tender. Avoid overcooking. Drain, saving hot water. Place starchy gems into large mixing bowl. Boil bacon eight minutes. Drain. Add all ingredients to mixing bowl. Blend well. Cover. Refrigerate. (Two hours minimum.)

"Another cheeseburger anyone?"

"Had enough son. Huge portions. Having trouble finishing this enormous installment. Thanks anyway."

"How about Jack? Care for more?"

"Probably should refrain. Already enjoyed two. Excellent flavor. Broiled to perfection. Occasionally, devour a well-made potato salad, but not very often. This version is the absolute tops. Forgot salt however."

"Grandma's recipe does not call for additional sodium chloride. Clogs arteries."

"Feeling alright Marlene? Been speechless all evening."

"Losing my best friend."

"Oh! So sorry. Must be tough. Your comrade dying?"

"No Carol. At least, I certainly hope not. He relocates far away soon. Very sad situation. Some distant place in western Saudi Arabia. Our pathways will most probably never cross again. Invested much time through several training years. Accepted Benji Rashad's latest $20,000 offer. Champion is sold."

# Outdoor fireplace.

Sunday July 25  2:15 p.m. Breathless Marlene met us in Linpav's parking area.

"Good afternoon. Taking up jogging?"

"Come quickly.  Follow me. Hurry. She is gorgeous. Energetic too."

"Who might that be?"

"Champion's daughter. Have not officially named her. Was born early this morning. Shortly after midnight."

"Hmm. Midnight hey? Perfect handle for a black Arabian mare."

"Sachet resonates better. My foal ended up being what judges consider a black bay with perfect markings."

Scene ends. Reopens 35 minutes later as coalition ambled toward front entrance.

"See our garden? Coming along well. Help yourself. Grab salad ingredients. Much leaf lettuce, cucumbers, and summer squash ripened already. Picked several tomatoes so far. Potato foliage displays white flowers. Must await first frost before harvesting them along with globe turnips."

"Honey? Go apprehend our ice chest, then start cooking."

Someone opened entrance door.

"Thanks Jack. Like deep-fried vegetables?"

"Humph. Sounds gross. Never tried any. Surely will sample minute portions. Still working overtime?"

"Only Monday through Friday. 50 hours per week. Why? Looking for another weekend truck driver?"

"Keep your mouth shut. Will discuss issues later. Hi Carol. Thanks for calling yesterday. Anymore tomatoes ripen yet?"

"Only saw these five orange ones. All others require additional sunshine."

"Howdy son. Avoid rushing with food. We ate dinner late. Nearly 1:00 o'clock."

"Hi Ma. Heard about insurance perplexity. No rental car. Major let-down."

"Terrible shame. Swapped my latest transportation. Bought another Subaru Outback."

"Comparably equipped?"

"Nearly identical. Odometer registers eight miles. This one is pale green though."

"When can we see this pale green vehicle Althea?"

"Possibly next weekend. Should experience few technicalities transferring registrations. Will call by Thursday."

"Hey! Just thought of something. All ladies leave immediately. Carol can chauffeur both passengers 50 miles. Round trip naturally. Investigate Althea's new wheels, while Pukka mobilizes supper."

"Yes. Worthy plan. Please accompany us Jack."

"Would enjoy that, but excessive paperwork hovers over me presently. Drive carefully. Early still. Appraise  serving our evening meal around 6:00 o'clock. Agreeable?"

"Makes perfect sense."

"Certainly. Come along girls."

Brother-in-law held off further conversation until absolutely positive we were alone.

"Don't know where to begin. All three doctors agree. Marlene harbors suspicions. Surely you noticed changes in my appearance. Lost over 40 pounds. Hair keeps falling out. Just a matter of when. Maybe one year left. And that is only two scholarly opinions. Radiation treatments keep failing."

"Who else knows?"

"No one does. Except my oldest daughter, Julie. And now you."

"Anything I can do?"

"Naturally. Keep my secret."

"Including Carol?"

"Yes. Otherwise there would exist numerous dilemmas."

"Have life insurance?"

"Policy was canceled. Already exhausted health insurance limitation. The worst part was selling my faithful wife's magnificent stallion. Humph. Already spent all that money."

"Why inform me? I am merely a designer/draftsman. Oh! Appropriate headstone?"

"Already finalized all arrangements. Linpav's Construction Company still operates well. Continues erecting two dozen new modular homes yearly. Retain full access to heavy equipment, plus huge discounts at many stores. Would like building unique outdoor fireplace. Some sort of legacy. Much time needed designing it? And at what cost?"

"Quality efforts consume time. 11 maybe 12 days altogether. Masonry-labor included. $50."

"Per hour? Ridiculous!"

"Stutter? Tee he. Sorry. Appropriate figure quoted represents my total price. Fabricating preliminary schematics during lunch break tomorrow."

"Done deal. Jotting down shopping list. What should I purchase initially?"

"Five gallons pre-mixed refractory fireplace cement, 260 fire bricks, three yards of ¾ inch crushed stone, four yards processed sand. Six 80-pound bags: Portland concrete. Three bags of masonry lime. Steel plates: 3/8" x 4' x 65", (2) ¼" x 6" x 10' (2) 6-inch stainless steel pipes by 10' long each. Will also require catwalk. 4' x 6' long."

"Where did you ever locate those colossal steaks?"

"Williamstown supermarket. Ordered them special from their deli department. Also grabbed A1 sauce."

"Was informed that I was born in Springfield, Mass. Never knew my biological parents. Was raised in a foster home. After being cremated, undertakers position my ashes beside your dad and grandparents. Sometimes, find myself wondering about earthly family. They represent everything to me. Especially now."

"Attend Jehovah church services today?"

"Of course. Will continue preaching indefinitely. Possibly, another full year. Dying is part of life."

"Exactly correct. Psalms 116 verse 15. Simply precious."

"Where headed?"

"Getting late. Must prepare many items. Come lend help."

"Certainly. Where does assistant chef begin?"

"Cleanse your hands, turn fry-o-later on, adjust thermostat: 370 degrees, rinse off fresh-picked vegetables, then slice them ½ inch thick. Remain alert. Do not cut yourself. Dispense plates and silverware. Hurry. Already 4:50."

"Been awhile. Should we not get things rolling?"

"Already did. Russets are baking. Salad was made. Veggies fry quickly. Sirloins are ready for broiling. Women should show up anytime."

"Whew! Clairvoyance."

"Hi Honey. Returned safely. Tried out Althea's new wheels. Drove nine miles."

"Awesome!"

"Unregistered?"

"Negative Jack. Borrowed dealer plates. Nice car, but much larger than my Volkswagen Golf."

"Come here. Mix virgin olive oil with vinegar."

"Ok. This apple cider variety suffice?"

"Indubitably. Stand over here. Excellent. Hush. Once everyone becomes seated, we must talk. Privately."

"Consequential stuff?"

"Very important. Fabricate some excuse why we must adjourn."

"Message received. Understand fully. Humph. Must grab something quickly. Hand over that tall white plastic container. Thanks. Hey, everybody. Look what silly Hubby forgot. Sour cream. Anyone else care for red wine?"

"Left our bottle home darling. Prefer beer instead. Daylight still. Let's go get some."

"Agreed. Returning shortly folks. Enjoy supper event."

Seven minutes slip away. Pulling into package store parking lot.

"Well? Am prepared for important information."

"Follow me. Apprehend a chilled 6-pack of beer, while red wine gets located."

Standing at checkout register,

"40 ounce Utica Club?"

"Only cost $2. Ice cold."

Back in car,

"I love you Carol. Where do we stand financially?"

"House, land, entire estate, vehicles, everything?"

"Readily available cash."

"$13,300 aboard checking account. Nearly $69,000 comprises our life savings."

"Trust your husband?"

"Totally. Love you Pukka."

6:25 p.m. Back at supper table,

"Set out stemmed glasses Big Sis. Hey Jack. De-cork this bottle."

"Cabernet sauvignon? Wow! $38."

"Contains resveratrol. Has beneficial properties. Heart benefits actually. Prevents fat cells from maturing."

"Prefer beer personally. Here Ma. Accept this endowment. Everyone needs dark-ruby colored medication."

"Only within moderate limitations Pukka."

"Exactly. Moderation is the key."

"Pleasant bouquet. Delicious."

"Sis? Estimate your newborn foal's monetary value."

"Never! Not for sale. Excessively immature still anyhow. Why?"

"Oh, Really? Priceless hey? Fact is, some close relative seeks substantial tax write-offs. $6,000 enough?"

"Humph. Interesting offer, but entirely unacceptable. Champion is her dad."

"I want that horse. Desperately. No rush. Couple years. Train Sachet for me. $8,000. Never mind. Make it $10,000 cash."

"Whew! Sure could use money."

"Darling? Make out appropriate bill-of-sale with proper check number included. $11,000. Act quickly."

"Sorry. Can not accommodate your request immediately."

"Reason being?"

"Ill equipped presently. Have no suitable paper."

"While Sis locates that item, please dispense wine refills. Would like proposing a special toast."

"Sure Pukka."

9 minutes slip away. Everyone raised their glass.

"To Momma's new car. May it prove luckier than her last."

Another brief moment slides oblivion bound.

"Seems accurate. Numbers coincide. Issuing warning, however. If your check bounces, our deal is canceled. There. Officially signed. Done bartering. Sold."

"Wait! Who pays retention fees? Safe haven, nutriments, veterinarian and farrier bills?"

"Pukka's horse now. My responsibilities. Darling? Produce another check. $2,000 this time."

Carol shakes her head, but complies.

"Here Marlene. First yearly maintenance installment. Keep all receipts. Should funds begin running low, call us. More will be supplied."

"Hmm. Time for another toast. Returning shortly."

Soon, my brother-in-law rebounds conveying milk-glass decanter.

"Been saving this for a very special occasion. 26 years old."

"Sorry. We never indulge with hard liquor."

"Italian red wine called: Barbaresco."

"Try some if you like. I am driving."

"Count me in. Still have any beer left?"

"Plenty. Over half-full still."

Shortly thereafter everyone stood poised with beverage raised.

"Grown accustomed. Routinely minister several hours. That scenario usually occurs in Kingdom Hall. This is not a speech or sermon. Been fortunate and understandably thankful. Only atheists live for the present. Perhaps, our savior will return soon. Here is to God's precious love."

"Care to spend the night with us?"

"Can't. Work beckons. Sachet needs your expertise. Strong bloodline. Train her well."

Wednesday July 28 5:35 p.m. Wife arrives home. Leaves engine running.

"Hop aboard."

"Sure. Let's beat feet. Call ahead?"

"Unnecessary. Left work an hour early."

"Not readily visible. Humph. Bring three extra-large pizzas?"

"Behind back seat. Pepperoni-hamburg, plain cheese, hot pepper-extra onion."

Scene ends. Reopens 20 minutes later, on familiar Stamford turf.

"Grabbing 12-pack. Carry everything else."

"Good evening Momma. Saw your car occupying driveway space."

"Howdy son, Carol. Did not feel like cooking tonight, hey?"

"Insufficient time. Jack here?"

"Downstairs probably. Check his study."

"Located where?"

"Just walked right past tan entrance door. Over there. Your left-hand side."

**"Go, while women discuss various topics. Want Coors light?"**

"Not yet. Setting these boxes here. Dining table. Help yourself. Enjoy chatting."

"Welcome to my studio. Perfect timing."

"Hi Jack. Interrupting anything?"

"Nah. Merely researching-composing Sunday's church sermon. What is this?"

"Find out. Unroll various illustrations. Represents three hours labor."

"Ordered everything on shopping list. They deliver steel plates tomorrow."

"Excellent. Inspect sketch #3. Make arrangements and weld accordingly. Dig an appropriate foundation orifice also."

"8' x 10'. Hmm. 40" deep?"

"Must get below frost line. Have access to huge limestone rocks?"

"How big?"

"Between 30 and 120 pounds. Will not use them all, but require roughly seven ton."

"Certainly. Next week soon enough?"

"Fine. Need 3/4 or inch thick plywood. (2) 8' long and (2) 10' specimen. Four sheets altogether."

"For framing apparently."

"Exactly. Let's adjourn. Brought some pizza."

# Sachet and sugar cubes.

Friday July 30 5:35 p.m. Phone rings.

"Hello."

"Hi Pukka. Jack calling. Stopping by tomorrow?"

"Yea. Early though. Before 9:00 o'clock."

"Great! Finished pouring cement yesterday about noontime. Big job. Foundation mandated 10 square yards."

"Been enterprising hey?"

"Very busy. Picked up catwalk, acetylene torch-tanks and Flux/cored MIG welder. Daylight still. Wondering. Could you possibly run over now?"

"Sure. Wife arrives momentarily. We will be there within half an hour. Bringing finalized detailed drawings."

Scene ends. Reopens at 8:45 p.m. Momma welcomes tired machinists.

"Howdy men. Starving?"

"Good evening Ma. Yes. Getting hungry."

"Famished myself. Accomplished much."

"Spending our night here? Why waste gasoline? Marlene invited us."

"Alright. Makes sense. Where is she anyway?"

" Laying down. Took Lyrica pills and Pepto-Bismol. Suffering recurring migraines. Experiencing nausea."

"Returning shortly. Checking on things."

"Steeping tea. Boiling two pounds of hot dogs. Chopping an onion."

"Need any assistance?"

"No son. Thanks anyway. Only obligate 20 or 25 uninterrupted minutes."

" Lets adjourn temporarily, purchasing foodstuff and some beer. Supposed to reach 95 degrees tomorrow."

"We are leaving Mom. Place supper on hold. Grabbing clean clothes. Should be back around 10:00."

"Past my bedtime. Will leave everything readily available. Avoid rushing through traffic. Drive safely. See you young folks later."

Saturday 7:40 a.m. Carol assisted making fresh brewed coffee, bacon, sausage patties, ten 8-inch buttermilk pancakes.

"Glad you could join us Sis. Did medication relieve your headache?"

"Feeling slightly better. Been diagnosed with fibromyalgia. Humph. Never even heard such terms before."

"Sounds serious. Where headed? Serving breakfast soon."

"Tending my treasured Arabians. Poses minor vexation actually. Will not involve much time."

Masons labored through lunch. By 6:30 firebox's inner core was nearing completion. Stood 40½ inches high. Lower grate and all six stainless ventilation pipes rested in their permanent locations.

"Open another refractory grout tub, then take a break. Place some phone calls. Recruit muscular volunteers. Must somehow position upper plate. Coordinate efforts. Inform these individuals be here at 8:00 o'clock sharp."

45 minutes later Carol welcomes our presence.

"Hi guys. Be seated. Start with fresh-picked salad. Want your Guinness now?"

"Certainly. Two black bottles. Glasses also. Boil that whole corned beef brisket?"

"Followed your instructions precisely. Onions, carrots, potatoes, cabbage. Construction advancing outdoors?"

"Made fantastic progress. Nearly all done for today darling. Hmm. Why displaying such a gloomy irremediable expression Jack? Dislike bitter distinct flavor?"

"Beer tastes great! Simply concerned. Think we applied enough adhesive compound between bricks?"

"Stop fretting. Employed plenty. Five millimeters thick. Glue represents weakest link anyhow."

"Whew! Hefty platter! Honey? Please come deliver sliced meat while I convey both teeming vegetable bowls."

Someone's vehicle horn beeps recognition.

"Our cue Pukka. Muscleman awaits explicit directions."

"Let's go elevate that monster. How many of us will be hoisting?"

"Three able bodies altogether. Third musketeer's name is Tiny. He weighs over 500 pounds."

Sunday July 31 11:15 a.m. Jack and my sister return from Kingdom Hall.

"Hi Carol. Mixing cement hey?"

"Yes Marlene. Been out here all morning. Fireplace is taking shape. This side nears completion. Look alright?"

"Fantastic! Who lifted all those humongous boulders?"

"Strong-armed Hubby. Will be quitting soon.  Two maybe 2½ more hours. Our Christian Harvest church praises begin shortly after that."

"Must change into old duds. Be right back."

Scene ends. Reopens Wednesday 8:30 p.m. Momma fried cabbage pirogues which she served with fresh beet greens and meatloaf. Additional company arrives.

"Good evening. Really awesome limestone structure. Working tomorrow?"

"Negative dear. Using another vacation day. Forecasters predict bright sunny episodes. Bring our suitcase?"

"Yes. Even remembered your electric razor. Left tan beast outside though. Behind car's back seat."

"Let's go purchase some beer before they close."

"Unnecessary maneuver. 12-pack of Natural Ice resides beside suitcase."

During supper Big Sis almost ruins everything.

"Ordered the special shiny item yesterday."

"Great! Almost time to tend Arabians. Right? I will go with you. Must check out young Sachet."

"Very intelligent foal. High spirited. Responds when I call her. Loves sugar cubes."

"Planning on lining fireplace's chimney with clay?"

"No Jack. Thanks for reminding me. Have access to 18-inch diameter 11 gauge stainless steel pipe? Could use a five-foot long specimen, plus two 1/4 inch thick face rings."

"That standard size?"

"Absolutely. 1/8 inch wall thickness. 24.09 pounds per linear foot."

"Too late tonight, but I will place some phone calls first thing tomorrow morning. Where are you going?"

"Apprehending our suitcase. Come along Mar. Where might sugar cubes be located?"

# Lasting Legacy.

Thursday August 4 7:45 a.m. Clean-shaven guest monopolized Linpav's entire kitchen area alone. Someone investigates.

"Howdy son. Little lady awake yet?"

"Sleeping late. Why not? Plans to call soon. Burning up one of her vacation days. Coffee must have brewed by now. Care for some?"

"Showering first. Microwave running?"

"Baking potatoes addressing home fries."

Momma leaves. Sausage patties, eggs benedict, home fries. Breakfast for five ravenous adults exemplified plenary success. My cheerful brother-in-law returns from his study revealing obvious contentment.

"Ah! Baring good news?"

"Located-purchased that pipe and supportive face rings. Foresee only one major predicament."

"Problem being?"

"Immediate delivery unavailable. Must wait eight or nine business days."

"Outer walls are nearing completion. Will be finished within six hours. Installing chimney two weeks from now."

Friday August 19 5:45 p.m. Carol transported our 12-pack of Amstel light bottles while I hauled teeming-full ice chest. No reason to ring chime. Door mystically opens upon our arrival.

"Welcome."

"Hello Marlene."

"Good evening. Supplied pasta components. Jack here?"

"Had another mysterious appointment. Never tells me where he goes, but expect his return momentarily."

"When should we dispense supper?"

"Boil jumbo shells beforehand, then stuff them with Ricotta cheese and bulk hot sausage. Bake collectivity one hour with much distinguishing spaghetti sauce. Serve everything at 9:00. Place beer in this ice chest right away."

"Where headed now?"

"Apprehending tan suitcase. Hey Mar! Grab something to collect vegetables in. Follow me."

Outside. Big Sis wanders toward garden patch.

"Might need high-polished ornament soon. Pick up that stainless steel commemoration yet?"

"Yesterday. Looks super. 5" high and 24" long. Cost $50."

"Here. Replenish your wallet. Gather salad ingredients. Leaf lettuce, cucumber, spinach, radishes, tender young edible pod peas, parsley. Send my wife out afterwards. She can help by operating cement mixer."

"Same proportions?"

"Exactly. One masonry lime, two Portland cement, six processed sand."

Host arrives.

"Hi. White fireplace is really taking shape. Where should I start?"

"Things are under control presently my friend. Get a notepad and pen to write these items down."

"Have both. Wait one minute. Ok. Go ahead."

"Require lumber: Dual 2 x 6's x 8 foot long, smallest roll of 3½ inch thick 15" wide fiberglass insulation. Oh! Duct tape also. Hmm. About 15 yards should suffice."

"Hardware Store remains open for another hour. Returning shortly."

Moments slip away.

"Almost 8:00 Honey. Must leave soon. Should pasta get baked without appropriate cover?"

"Employ tin-foil. Punch slots allowing hot air's escape though. 350 degrees sounds about right. Have fun."

Brother-in-law returns. Seems disappointed.

"Quitting already?"

"Hardly Jack. Daylight still. The night is young. Crank your welder up."

"Sure thing. Bought a razorblade knife."

Saturday August 20 9:45 a.m. Wooden staging rested 25 inches high aboard upper grate. Jack and I wrestled  positioning 135 pound chimney liner. Mixed cement. Hoisted several large limestones. Labored until 5:40. Fireplace appeared complete. Only one remaining technicality. Marlene arrives on cue with hefty cartage.

"Excellent timing Sis. Must keep our welder busy. Lasting legacies require sustenance."

"Check things out. Baby brother designed your permanent memoranda."

"Awesome! Stainless steel plaque reads: John (Jack) Linpav-2005"

"Weld it vertically centered on this faceplate. Hurry. Hear distant rumbling? Thunderstorm moves closer."

Scene ends. Reopens 7:30 p.m. Everyone was seated at supper table.

"Raining fiercely. Glad we covered my fireplace with blue plastic tarp."

Bing.

"What was that?"

"Just stove's timer signaling. Dumplings are ready. Come along Honey. Serve chicken stew."

"Wait! Here Pukka. Our agreed-on price. $50 cash."

"Thanks. Pull in two cord of firewood. Preferably cherry. After cement fully cures we will christen event."

Friday August 26 5:35 p.m. Arrived at Linpav's Arabian horse ranch.

"Hi Jack. Marlene or Althea around?"

"Not yet. Went shopping together. They left two hours ago."

"Brought oodles of stuff. Cookware mostly."

"Have supper yet?"

"Only tea. Made plenty. Might still remain warm. Care for some?"

"Not immediately. Must unpack truck's bed first. Supplied many useful cooking utensils-instruments."

"Need assistance with that endeavor?"

"Absolutely. Would save walking individual jaunts. Some items are capacious."

"Humph. Major understatement. Picnic table weighs a ton. Outdoor storage box poses heavy also."

20 minutes later.

"Did you build this sturdy table yourself?"

"Pukka designed/constructed everything employing stainless steel hardware. Only used pressure treated lumber. Should perpetuate through several harsh winters."

37 inch fireplace shovel, 28 inch poker, Butcher-block style steel brush, 10 gallon galvanized pail with handle and tight fitting lid, long-handled: Spatula, scoop, fork. Tin foil, 32 ounce squeeze bottle, large wicker basket, (8) Natural Rattan woven paper plate holders (100) 9" diameter paper plates, plastic forks, knives, 16-ounce Styrofoam cups, mitten style potholders.

"Remove blue tarp, unveiling your legacy Jack. After 6:00 already. Supper will not be ready for 70 minutes."

"Want me scouring potatoes?"

"Yes dear. Dress them in heavy gauge foil leaving one end open. De-husk corn, and then wrap all ears likewise."

"What are you squirting top surface with?"

"My special outdoor blend. Peanut oil, garlic powder, black pepper. Fire this beauty up. Getting hungry."

"Look! They are back."

"Good evening everyone. For my birthday boy. Your presents remain in car still. Nothing much."

"Awesome card. Thanks Ma."

"Let me read that. Wow! Time flies. 55 years old. Where headed Honey?"

"Already applied oil blend. Slipping these sealed gems under lower grate. Hot coals will bake them perfectly."

"Want beer now?"

"Yes. Apprehend our bulk package of chicken legs with thighs attached."

# Interesting theory.

Saturday August 27, 2005 7:45 a.m. Jack and Marlene investigate their kitchen area.

"Not positive about color preference or exact shoe size, but these light tan beauties should fit."

"Happy birthday Pukka."

"Wow! Leather moccasins. Beautiful. Thanks."

"Best tasting chicken I ever had. Corn was delicious. Want limestone fireplace cranked up again presently?"

"Sounds appropriate. Let's go. Hey Sis. Stay behind. Inform everyone 9:00 o'clock breakfast."

Scene ends. Reopens 8:20 a.m. Women locate picnic table seats. Momma offers keys.

"Walk to my Subaru. Black plastic bag belongs over here. Remain alert. Fragile contents."

"Sure. Be right back."

Moments slip away. Marlene tended Arabian horses. Curious plastic bag rests aboard tabletop.

"Returning Subaru keys."

"Super! Now open birthday presents. Both are identical."

"What did smiling Hubby get?"

"Twin super high dome lids. Boxes claim 11 inch diameter. Excellent. Tempered glass. Thanks Ma. How would you like eggs cooked?"

"Sunny side up. Employ topical cookware dome."

"Runny yolks?"

"Yes. Dislike them dry."

Sausage links, bacon, eggs, toast, coffee. Breakfast personified total success. Subsequent clean-up was easy.

"Let's journey home. Should check our mailbox."

"Ok. Probably have answering machine messages Need my electric razor. Grab tan suitcase."

"Also require our ice chest. Address that issue. Will undoubtedly come in handy."

Soon, departure time was inevitable. Carol waved, hopped aboard passenger seat.

"Bye everyone. Returning tomorrow late afternoon. After church services. Hmm. About suppertime."

Sunday 5:35 p.m. Wife parked beside someone's blue Ford Focus. Apparently Linpav's entertained company. We unpacked food items. Blonde young lady approaches.

"Hi uncle Pukka. See my new wheels?"

"Amy? Wow! How you have grown. Nearly as tall as your dad these days. Nice car. Hope you enjoy shellfish."

"Like hard-shell clams, oysters, mussels. Love jumbo Alaskan king crab legs. Lobsters are pretty good also."

"Great! Bought a bushel of cherrystone's yesterday afternoon. Soaked them in cornmeal overnight. They should not be gritty. Serving surf and turf for supper. Must empty ashes in Marlene's garden first though. Planned evening's meal at 7:00 o'clock. Hasten back admonishing intentions."

Steamers, melted butter, potato-egg salad, sirloin steaks. Everyone enjoyed their delightful supper. Momma, Amy and I readily devoured three teeming plates of clams apiece. All others were content with two helpings.

"Anyone care for fruit salad?"

"None for me. Had plenty."

"Appreciate the reminder. Honey? Apprehend our golden delicious basket, testing your theory."

"Look at that stash. Gorgeous yellow apples."

"Enough for every 4-legged friend out there. Follow me. Call Sachet up to their fence limit."

Big Sis did. Sachet responded immediately.

"Hello handsome Baby. Never ate one of these yet. Try one. They are softer than sugar cubes. Hey Marlene! She enjoys them even better. Aw. Pretty equine. True champion bloodline."

"Spending overnight visitation?"

"No. Must work tomorrow. Actually, we will be leaving soon."

"Concerned about Jack. He has been acting strange lately. Thinking another woman caught his eye."

"Stop fretting. Ordained ministers remain faithful. Keep an even keel. Well, let's rejoin festivities."

"Do not mention our conversation. Right?"

Friday 5:25 p.m. Checked empty mailbox. Proceeded up driveway.

"Welcome home. Supposed to rain heavily later tonight. Already confirmed Williamstown Supermarket flyer. Labor Day sale ends Sunday. Perhaps postponing 24 hours makes sense."

"But everything has been packed. We already formulated long weekend plans. Lock up and let's go."

"Grabbing my raincoat first. Want yours?"

"Guess so. Sound curriculum darling."

**6:45 p.m. Arrived at Linpav's estate. Grabbed both suitcases. Headed toward main entrance door.**

"Howdy son. Carol."

**"Good evening Althea."**

"Hi Ma. Glad your voice came back. Never suffered laryngitis myself. Must be frustrating."

"Humph. Major understatement. Lasted four days this occasion."

**"Anyone else here?"**

"Marlene. Not feeling well tonight though. Took Lyrica pills addressing fibromyalgia disaccords. Supposedly, two-timing husband returns from Mexico tomorrow afternoon."

"Avoid rushing conclusions. Sometimes things are different from their outward appearance."

"Know something we don't?"

"Yes. God created time, earth and the word. Realizing folly, he established various eternal heavens."

"Interesting theory."

# Already there.

Saturday September 3, 2005 4:45 p.m. Familiar blue Ford Focus arrives.

"Hi uncle Pukka. Sitting beside picnic table all alone?"

"Good afternoon Amy. Jack. Everyone else waits indoors. Visited Mexico?"

"Not me. Only dad and sister Julie. Returning later. Must tell my mother something."

"Hungry yet?"

"Ate lunch on the jet hours ago."

Amy heads toward female reunion.

"What is up?"

"Experimental procedure. Unsanctioned in U.S.A. Probably will not work, but any chance is better than none."

"Marlene harbors suspicions. Thinks another woman might be involved."

"Serious? Humph. Well, least of my problems. Emptied fireplace ashes hey?"

"Sprinkled vitamins throughout garden. Provides beneficial nutrients. Care for beer? Brought several ice-packed specimen. Guinness extra. Help yourself. Red chest with white cover."

"Great idea. Oh! These bottles are not twist offs. Opener available?"

"Use my lighter. Lids pop off readily."

"Really? Mind demonstrating?"

"Minor child's play."

"Wow! Who taught you that maneuver?"

"Grandpa. Hmm. 45 years ago. Only, he used many other items back then."

"George was highly intelligent. Been ages. Still remember him?"

"Who could ever forget lessons taught from such gifted individuals."

"Must go check in. Need a cushion anyway. Stoke up fireplace."

"Inform hungry folks. Serving our supper at 6:30."

Scene ends. Reopens punching 6:00 o'clock.

"Best start cooking son."

"Already did. Potatoes, corn, onions reside below lower grate. What would Ma like for main course? Steak, fish, pork loin, or chicken halves?"

"Had fish and chips recently. What version of beef did master chef purchase?"

"Rib eyes. Eight-ounce gems. Porterhouse beauties also. Enormous 1¼ pound giants with tails included."

"Chicken tasted superb last week. Will stick with that."

"Excellent choice. Same here."

"Whooping 3-inch thick slice of pork loin sounds good Honey."

"No problem. Me too."

"Awesome, baby brother! Many profound choices. Hmm. Rib eye."

"Name your preference Amy."

"Really famished tonight. Porterhouse steak. Medium-rare."

"Great! Poses minimal inconvenience."

"Why venture so far south Jack?"

"Carol? Come lend helping hands. Slice lengthy pork loin."

Added four more chunks of cherry firewood. Away from the crowd private conversation developed.

"Was merely curious. Marlene wanted to know."

"Mind your own business. Let God work things out."

"Magnificent design Pukka. Chimney works perfectly."

"Glad you are happy with unorthodox fireplace. Help yourself. Grab another bottle of stout."

"We playing cards later? Texas Hold em or Polish pitch?"

"Only card game I know is cribbage, but willing to learn."

"Unnecessary frustration. Cribbage it will be. $2 apiece per game. No skunks. Cut for partners."

Sunday 4:35 p.m. Arrived at Linpav's estate. Added solitary bag of ice cubes aboard each chest. Emptied wood ashes. Carted bushel basket filled with Golden Delicious apples toward white retaining fence. Imitated Marlene's clicking sound.

"Sachet! Come investigate. Oh! Very fleet-footed smart handsome pony. Your scrumptious reward."

"Hi uncle. Hey Mom. Look at all those yellow apples."

"Yes Amy. Impressive. Awesome, baby brother! Fruit looks pristine."

"Grab some. Many hungry mouths anticipate. This represents only a small portion, Supplied many tasty gems. Seven teeming bushel altogether. Various treats. Cortland mostly. Macintosh, Granny Smith. Bartlet plus Honey Sweet pears also. Will commence lugging remaining specimen over yonder, stockpiling red storage barn."

**Scene ends. Reopens 30 minutes later. Everyone was gathered around picnic table area.**

"Dad? Jehovah witness screening process uncover anyone suitable yet? Am old enough to start dating."

"Remain patient another month or more. Life-long commitment. Your marriage takes place soon enough."

"We playing cribbage after supper? If so, can Carol be my partner again? Won $8 last night. She is lucky."

**"Yes. Same teams. Right Althea?"**

"Works for me. Caught us by two elusive pegs both times. Hey, look! Massive wingspan. Giant soaring eagle."

"Wrong assumption. Large beauty lives on fish. They are called osprey. Must have some nearby lake."

"That would be Somerset Reservoir. Miles away though. He will be attaining…. Humph. He is already there."

# Birthday bash.

Monday September 5, 2005 10:45 a.m. Momma locates her seat at busy picnic table. Everyone else except Marlene was already seated. Older Sis was within shouting distance while tending black Arabian horses.

"How are things progressing job-wise Pukka? Read an article in this morning's newspaper. Apparently, your outfit is for sale."

"Really Ma? Well, matters little anyway. Was offered another local position. Pittsfield. Last week. Significant pay raise."

"How things change. Will my son be designing paper product machinery there?"

"No. Plastic injection molds. Interesting stuff. Hmm. Was considering my resignation actually."

"Must be well off financially. Two person family. Awesome incomes. Definitely old enough. Why not retire?"

"Barely 55 currently. Plan struggling another ten years."

"Feeling alright Dad? Look awfully pale."

Scene ends. Reopens 57 minutes later. North Adams Regional Hospital's emergency room.

"Will my husband be alright?"

"Cancer has spread. Nothing we can do. He has refused admittance. Insists on returning home. Wants to die in peace. Please sign this waiver overriding irrational suicidal behavior. We could keep him sedated here."

"Not endorsing your hopefully bogus determination, or signing any such paperwork"

12:49 p.m. Back at Linpav's estate.

"Getting hungry. Stoke up the white limestone fireplace."

"Sure darling. Serving lunch punching 1:20. Much food remains. Go pick fresh veggies, then make another big garden salad. Do not spare virgin olive oil."

"May I be of any assistance?"

"Absolutely. Need one pint of kerosene hastening flames. Tight schedule."

"Diesel fuel suffice? Have plenty."

"Perfect! Only require six or eight ounces."

"Poses little inconvenience. Returning shortly. Oh! Almost forgot. Here Pukka. Now we are square."

"Thanks. Just love $50 bills."

Jack Linpav passed away 17 days later. Marlene lost entire estate along with her best friend. Sold all horses at a public auction. Daughter, Julie, renovated her basement. Constructed an efficiency apartment for her newly homeless mother. Nice small apartment, but nothing like prior living quarters. Luckily, Julie owned a large field where big sis could pursue training Sachet. By late August of 2006 gorgeous black bay was proving its worth. Won five regional championships out of as many entered. Why not? Magnificent piece of horseflesh. Strong family tree. Very intelligent. Talented enough to win in Kentucky? Wrong. Only mustered second place. Hmm. History has a way of repeating itself. Was offered $18,500 cash from same Saudi Arabian buyer.

7:30 Saturday evening September 23: Phone rang three times before Carol could answer.

"Hello."

"Hi. Baby brother there? Just received another counter offer for Sachet. $25,000 plus expenses."

"Not home yet. Still working ten hour days. Will have him call you back."

"When? Tonight?"

"Due anytime now. Will have him return your message within… Hmm. 15 minutes or so."

Managed to accumulate 20 hours overtime for the week. Plodded up front stairway.

"Welcome home. Call your sister."

"Which one? Beverly? Surprise party canceled? Momma alright?"

"Everything remains unchanged. Call birthday girl, but do not ruin anything. Hurry though. Meatloaf is ready."

"Baked potatoes?"

"Yes. Fresh ears of corn also. Only boiled five of them. Saving all others anticipating celebration bash."

"Robert and Donna showing up?"

"Naturally. Everyone will be there."

"Super. Entire family get together. Can hardly wait."

Sunday September 24, 2006 11:45 a.m. Arrived at Beverly's house. Many vehicles cluttered her driveway so Carol parked silver transportation on the lawn. No need to ring entranceway's chime. Door magically opens.

"Great! Set those items on kitchen table."

"Sure Althea. Supplied fresh corn. Notice my new wheels? Hubby bought me another new Volkswagen Golf. Last one was getting tired. Hubby worked out an awesome deal."

"Nice looking rig. Should have purchased a Subaru though, but each to his own."

"Excellent gas mileage. 40 miles per gallon. Hi Marlene. Hope you are enjoying this special day."

"Brought a cold 12-pack of Coors light. Noontime already. Having mine immediately. Anyone else care for some?"

Learned several items. Beverly served lunch punching 1:30 p.m. Delightful spaghetti sauce, rigatoni, lobsters, corn. After eating, Momma delivered double-layered cake laced with candles. Big sis made her wish and blew them out. By 3:00 o'clock every present had been addressed. All except our unique gift.

"Here. Not much. Open light box."

"Feels empty. Some type of practical joke?"

"No joke. There is an envelope inside."

"This is your original bill-of-sale."

"Really? May I see that one minute?"

"Ok."

"Absolutely positive about this Honey? Humph. Guess so."

"Hey! Be careful! You are tearing it."

"Yes. Into many tiny pieces."

"Sachet belongs to you now. Happy birthday Marlene."

# Crimson wishes.

Sunday morning October 1, 2006 niece, Julie, helped us pick apples and pears until 11:30. Sold all but seven bushel to Rita at Norman's Variety store later that early afternoon. Collected whapping $252. Attended 2:00 o'clock church services. Returned home punching 3:45.

"Cooking supper tonight? Worn out. Wife resembles someone totally exhausted."

"No problem darling. Plan making french fries, ground sirloin with mushroom-laced brown gravy. Sound at all enticing?"

"Excellent. They will undoubtedly taste delicious. Hear something? A door closed outside."

"Hi again. Stopped back to grab my extension ladder and three baskets of luscious apples as agreed."

"Hello Julie. Hubby can assist you with that project. I am thoroughly beat Honey. Awaken me when our evening meal nears completion."

"7:00 o'clock seem about right?"

"Perfect. Do not make excessive noise until then."

Carol exits.

"Let's run downstairs grabbing that ladder."

"Should be simple enough. Brought my truck. How is yours running these days?"

"Getting old. Purchased another. They are building my new rig presently. King cab, beefed up suspension, loud horn, extra heavy-duty alternator, 4" lift kit, auxiliary lights, sliding rear view window, fiberglass cap,  etc. "

"Wow! What did you buy? Another full-sized pickup?"

"No. Gas prices are ridiculous. This is a smaller 4-wheel drive version. Short bed only measures 6' 4". Harbors fuel injected 6-cylinder engine. Must wait 15 more days to take Ford Ranger's delivery."

"Automatic transmission?"

"Five-speed standard with overdrive."

"How will you haul your camper around?"

"Already sold that albatross. Got paid $950 cash. Staying for supper? Nothing special tonight. Hamburgers."

"No. Working six days per week. Must get going soon. Alarm clock buzzes early every day. Wishing good luck with both new vehicles."

"Thanks Julie. Drive carefully."

"Always do. Bye uncle."

Upstairs 6:55 p.m.

"Wake up darling. Sleep later. Supper is ready."

"Whew! Must gain composure. Hmm. Get her apples? She still here?"

"Went home with three baskets-full hours ago. Come along. Must flip broiling meat."

Monday October 16: Arrived at Beverly's driveway approaching 6:20 p.m.

"Hi Carol, Nice to see you guys. Good looking truck brother. Wish I had money like that. Running behind schedule. Was just leaving. Mom waits inside the house. Departing immediately. Stupid union meeting. Enjoy."

"Returning anytime soon?"

"Not likely. Robert might show his face. Bye."

Shortly thereafter we three musketeers were situated in Beverly's parlor. Seated aboard her reclining chair, Momma appeared astounded for some unknown reason.

"Small gas saver hey? Looks big to these old eyes. Probably will not get even 20 miles per gallon."

"Probably right about that, but sticker claims 22. Do not drive very far these days anyhow."

"Difficult believing those foolish stickers sometimes. Getting dark outside. Otherwise we could take a spin."

"Beverly mentioned Robert might stop over."

"Bobby labors constantly same as his dad. Never shows up when important issues develop. Was supposed to inspect our clogged kitchen sink tonight."

"Anything Pukka can fix?"

"Guessing no way. Job requires pipe wrenches. Humph. Could cure the problem myself allotted proper tools."

"Hey! Someone showed up. Probably Bobby."

Door swings open.

"Good evening. Well, don't look so happy to see me."

"Hello Marlene. Thought you might be someone else."

"Hmm. Makes sense. Robert called from Otis. He digs foundations there. Brought two of his pipe wrenches."

"Perfect! Your cue Honey. Go unclog kitchen's drain."

**Scene ends. Reopens 20 minutes later.**

"There. Problem solved. Be sure Robert gets these tools back."

"No difficulty. Oh! Sold my glamorous Sachet. Needed cash."

**"Obviously made you sad."**

"Yes. Feel deserted again. Lost Champion, plus 18 other fabulous Arabians."

"Been years, but I remember exercising your very first quarter horse. Oh, can not recall names."

"Willow Wisp. Who could ever forget such treasures? Handsome golden Palomino. Wrote a poem about him."

**"Recently?"**

"Long ago Carol. Was actually some English project during college."

"Very interesting. Would enjoy reading this poem someday. Have any title?"

"Crimson wishes."

# Renovated core pin.

Wednesday October 18 @ 7:10 p.m. Placed crucial phone call:

"You have contacted Hartwig residence. Leave a message."

"Good evening Earl. Pukka Carpenter calling. Today …"

"Hello buddy."

"Hi Earl. Been awhile. How are you faring these days?"

"Humph. Grown tired of complaining. Fair to middling. Wheel chair confined. Experiencing problems with these useless legs. Tough growing old."

"True. Busy tonight? We could take a skip over visiting. Have another small job."

"Getting late. Am settled in for the evening. Drop by Sunday morning after 10:00. Bring lunch."

"Magnificent plan. Oh! Would you like a small half-pint bottle of blackberry brandy?"

"Quit drinking hard liquor altogether. Please do not supply any. Doctor's orders. Beer is alright. Can consume small quantities in moderation."

Sunday 11:35 a.m. Artist reads through Marlene's poem.

"Anyone care for more decaffeinated tea?"

"None here. Two cups was plenty. Nearly noon already. Miller time. Grab three cans, then warm our pizza."

"Cold beer sounds agreeable. Pizza would be tasty also."

King Earl locates his pen. Starts sketching. 40 minutes slip away.

"All done. This Willow Wisp must have been quite impressive."

"Beautiful horse. Powerful. Quick. Responsive. Oh! He had heart."

"Looks fantastic! Rabbit, squirrel, four soaring birds. Six of God's lovely creatures altogether. How much owed addressing your artwork?"

"Free labor young lady. Was pleasurable."

After church services, hastened over sister Beverly's house.

"Howdy son, Where is Carol?"

"Doing our laundry. Dropped her off home. Formulate any supper plans yet?"

"Have chicken defrosting in the refrigerator. Why?"

"We are planning to hit some restaurant. Promising opportunity for riding as passenger aboard my new truck."

"What time?"

"Not hungry presently. Hmm. How does 6:00 o'clock sound?"

"Hmm. Four hours from now. Ok. Dress full tilt?"

"Neither of us are. Beverly working? Invite her also."

"Naturally. Cooking until 7:00. Acquiring groceries afterward."

"Too bad. Perhaps Marlene could attend."

"Will investigate that strong possibility. Am positive my oldest sibling would like that."

"Utilize your phone. Leaving directly."

Shortly thereafter, poor Pukka was locked out from his house. Sign on door read: 'Wet surface. Go around'.

"Sorry for any inconvenience. Just waxed kitchen's floor."

"Minor impropriety. Should probably call ahead, solidifying reservations somewhere?"

"Let's play things by ear. Early still. Beverly coming?"

"Unable. Very busy tonight. Stopping for groceries on her way back from work, but my other sister possibly joins our troupe."

"Great! She can keep me company on rear bench seat."

"Do not have one darling."

"Joking? Where are we supposed to sit? Rationalized your $14,800 king cab pickup with no rear bench seat? Whew! Business settled. Taking my Volkswagen. Much greater passenger capacity. Better gas mileage. Wiser choice."

"Wrong. Ordered two thickly padded flip-down jump seats. Both equipped with safety belts. Relax."

"Your truck stands high off the ground. Althea could experience troubles climbing aboard. Offer assistance."

Parking lot was full. Luckily, someone exited close to entrance door. Waited in line nearly 20 minutes. Each ordered similar meals (Rib-eye steak and baked potato), then attacked Bonanza's salad-soup bars.

"Here son, twin $10 bills."

"Leave one of those for a tip later. Already informed everyone supper is on me."

"Ok. Thanks."

"Say what Marlene? Did not catch that."

"Heading back for more corn chowder. Everything tastes very good, but not delicious like meals cooked aboard Jack's legacy."

**Carol and big sis adjourn.**

"Like my new truck Momma?"

"Immensely. Payments must be atrocious."

"Do not have any. Managed spectacular cash deal. Saved a few thousand bucks."

"Job secure?"

"None ever are. In order to remain competitive in today's marketplace all employees constantly struggle with corporate downsizing."

"What does my son design at Starr Technologies?"

"Many interesting items actually. Bottle caps, plastic pens, etc. Am presently renovating prevalent core pins."

"Reinventing the wheel hey?"

"Present versions perform alright, but experience short life spans. Possibly, many months. Unsure still. My new rendition should last several years."

Printed in the United States
By Bookmasters